AF815001

BE

by
Eldon Taylor

Publisher's Cataloging in Publication
(Prepared by Quality Books Inc.)

Taylor, Eldon.
Be / by Eldon Taylor.
p. cm.
ISBN: 1-55978-782-1

I. Title.

PS3570.A956B4 1996 813'.54
QBI96-20331

Editing by Tony Markham

© 1994 Eldon Taylor
Printed 1997
All rights reserved.
No part of this book may be reproduced
in any form or by any means without
permission in writing from the publisher.
R.K. Books
557 California St., Suite 118
Boulder City, NV
89005

TEL: 1-800-964-3551

ISBN 1-55978-782-1

To the purpose of life,
the mystery of strife,
the shadow of dark,
the voltage of light;
to black versus white,
the waste in our work,
come visions in the night—
Love is Life's Perfect Sight.

To Roy

About The Author

Eldon Taylor is President of Progressive Awareness Research, an organization founded to discover and develop techniques for self empowerment. He calls himself a cowboy philosopher. His enthusiasms include science, philosophy, poetry and horse breeding. He fundamentally believes in life as a school and the human condition as inherently endowed with the power to enjoy and apply vast potentials beyond our dreams. These convictions led him to doctorates in both Pastoral and Clinical Psychology.

He emphasizes the use and results of science and philosophy. "If it doesn't work, the finest theory or philosophy needs changing!" Universities in the US and Germany have tested the patented "Taylor Method" of cognitive behavioral modification. Experimental results have proven his approach to be effective.

Many leading biographic publications include Eldon, notably the Who's Who of Intellectuals, Who's Who Among Human Service Professionals and Who's Who of Science and Engineering. Many newspapers and magazines have referred to his research. Omni featured his work with subliminal communication in their anniversary audio experience. He has made hundreds of radio and television appearances. His original double blind studies in prison systems were prompted after working 12 years in criminology and criminalistics.

INTRODUCTION

Like many, I came to a point in my life where too little had meaning. Every day meant simply the same old routine. It was like I had done all of the things that I dreamed of doing and/or had given up the dream.

This is an empty point where life has lost its purpose and enthusiasm is something remembered like a childhood experience. The questions regarding life's meaning burn constantly in your head. It's a time when a little retrospect reveals the emotional casualties that could easily have been avoided. It's the time when most search for meaning. Who am I and what is being? How do I be me, whatever that means?

I wished that some all wise-mentor would appear and provide the answers. I had recently attended an event where the petite and lovely J. Z. Knight channeled an almost too powerful Ramtha. Ramtha, an ascendant warrior from Neanderthal days, seemed to come right at me speaking only bottom lines. No frills and no hocus-pocus. Someone to illuminate the shadows, to clarify the ambiguous, to put your talk and feelings to work, wouldn't that be nice. Then one day I thought, "Yes—but with my luck the wise one would be just some old wise ass playing with me." That is when the idea for this book came to me. "This would make a great story, some confused professional who has done most of the things he set out to do only to find that they were of little consequence. Make him the skeptic that I am and give him a guide who appears and channels information through him. Except, the disembodied spirit won't be a serious channel, he'll be a prankster."

I started the story. Without an outline. This was to have been something that I would write just for me, a therapeutic way to vent some feelings. However, what happened took on a different direction. When I set up the framework and started the dialogue, something took over. I would take a question to the keyboard and the Dink, the comic channeler, would give me an answer.

Many of the questions were being asked of me, for I had agreed to teach *A Course In Miracles*. The Course had changed my life and teaching it constantly tested both my understanding and the depth of change. I was disappointed in myself, for the change seemed much shallower than I wished to admit. Thus, my dialogues with the Dink served many purposes.

Is the Dink a part of my own psyche? Is he the **trickster** within that Jung speaks of? Is he some aspect of consciousness, or super-consciousness, or collective unconsciousness that I tapped in to? I can't answer that. What I know is that the answers given me were somehow outside of me, yet always in a context with which I was familiar.

Whatever the source, the book did not come entirely from what I know as me. The ending was my wife's idea, both its time and method. But even the conclusion seemed to be known by some level of myself, or the Dink, for it was pre-written into the dialogues the Dink and I had before the suggestion was made. The answers given me have been meaningful for those who have read the book thus far. I hope they have value to you. Who wrote the book is academic if the content serves.

Thank you.

CHAPTER ONE

Goals

I can look at where I am,
compare it to where I want to be,
set my goals
and work to be there for me.
OR,
I can look at what I ***be****,*
accept that what I ***be*** *is me,*
change my goals
so that what is me is what I ***be****.*
OR,
Is what is me
not good enough for me to be?
OH,
To be ***and*** *not to* ***be****.*

As the sun set behind the polluted California skies—I thought what beauty in the panoramic color prisiming through particulate matter.

"It's purty cuz it shines through such shit."

I refused to acknowledge the comment from the voice behind me for I felt that although the observation was correct, it simply spoiled what beauty there was to behold. Perhaps, I thought, a cynical person finds only the ghastly in life while others, like myself, searched for the beauty, the good in all.

"*Good*—my friend, don't you know *good* is as much an illusion as *bad*?"

Startled that this last comment was so sychronistic with my thoughts, I turned around to face its author. I was alone on the hilltop. No one was there.

"So, you're hearing voices my *good* fellow. Does that make you feel *bad*?"

I jerked back around to meet the voice that had moved around me when I turned. But still no one was there.

"Hey guy, you're going to hurt yourself spinning around like that."

"Okay, I give. Where are you?"

"Easy question, hard answer. I was bored so I decided to find some open, good seeking kinda person, and give us both a little exercise in that channeling business."

"What do you mean 'channeling'?"

"Easy guy, don't get riled. Consider yourself lucky. I'm gonna give ya' some hints on the secrets of life. Ain't that why ya' drove all the way up here?"

"Let me see if I have this straight, you're some disembodied being and you want to come through me in order to enlighten the world. Have I got that right?"

"Right on guy! As I said—You should be so lucky. No . . . no Ramtha Schmantha for you fella."

"I like—like I like the idea of you finding someone else. Or like, I'll just leave now and later I'll work out whether this was a delusion, an instance of bicamerality, some latent schizophrenic tendency, or as you say, whatever."

With that, I started back toward my automobile.

"Hey wait guy. All those possibilities you just spit out and you missed the obvious one—it's me, not you that's speaking here."

"Sure," I muttered without shortening my stride.

"Stop dude! I'll prove it."

The temptation was too great, I stopped.

"Okay, now lookit here. From my perspective, there just ain't much to do. I never fancied myself as some spirit in this dimension of spirits all looking to do good. I just sort of happened here. I mean, I spent my last life on earth raising a little hell and having a lot of fun, and then this here kid he got in trouble. Well, I rescued him; you know, saved his life. Weren't much . . . It was cold and wet and a lot of people yelling encouragement from the edge of the busted ice. Damned if it didn't kill me though. Well, the reward is this here stuff, or place, and ya' know, I'm gettin' mighty tired of it and thinking about comin' back into where you are. Now the damned thing is that you're where I want to be and I'm where you want to be. Right?"

"You mentioned proof?"

"I just gave ya' some. Lookit here. You stopped your car and came out on this hill just to look at what you think is a marvel of nature, 'God's beauty manifested before your eyes'. Now ain't that right? Tell me those weren't your thoughts."

"Go on."

"Yeah, well, you been thinkin' that there are two things in your life that are working. Namely your relationship with God and your relationship with your wife. Right?"

"Stop here for a minute. Instead of you telling me of me, tell me something about you."

"Well, like I said guy, I ended up here because of one damned self sacrificin' thing I did. I'd do it again. I mean a fellow's got to be who he is, do what he's got to do. Some things ya' just do 'cause that's how you're made."

"What's your name?"

"My last earthly name was Dunken D. Dingle, but most folks just called me Dink."

Dink, I thought. Serves me right. I'd read a little about so-called channels. I'd even had a patient convinced she was channeling an energy she called Hermes. Hermes, the great Hermes himself. Oh, but I get Dink.

"Now listen. Remember that I know your thoughts. And that last batch was kinda insultin'. I may not've been a Hermes, but I'll tell you what, the folks over here ask a whole lot more of me then they do some of those so-called great philosophers and teachers."

"Really. Why is that—Dink?"

It's simple guy, I lived my last life with gusto. I like that word, don't you?"

"Gusto—what's that supposed to mean? I'll tell you what it means to me, a beer commercial on television. You only live once—they lie—so do it with gusto. Burn out those synapses, get drunk, party, forget reality and lose those inhibitions. What nonsense."

"Nonsense? Let me tell you a story about gusto. Seems these two here fellas were on earth. They knew each other in the prior life, but didn't know that here on earth. Well one of them just be'ed. You know, he just lived as he was. No bullshit. No mental games with himself. He let his feelings tell him who he was. Hell, he'd ride all night in a snow storm, near like freezin' his capute off. You know, capute—his hind end. Well anyhow, back in the bunk house in front of that old pot belly stove, he'd tell about that storm. Why his face would light up with joy as he went back over that night. You'd even see terror in his eyes when he told of comin' down the old switch-back with its sheer falloffs on both sides. You'd feel his anxiety as he described his pony slippin' almost over the edge, scramblin' to get his feet back under him. He'd take this experience full of bitter ass cold, frozen fingers, dumb ol' cows, near fallin' to his death, and make it the most excitin' thing you ever listened to. Lot's of young buckaroos, includin' myself wanted to be just like him.

"Well one day he met this here other fella. Now his old buddy from the prior life was one of them there intellectuals. He was a college perfesser back East, I think somewhere in Boston. Anyhow, this perfesser fella came out West to study Indians. And one day, these two ol' buddies met up in the town bar. Now the perfesser was spinnin' yarns about the Indians 'cause he'd had a little too much to drink; and he wasn't accustomed to it ya' know. So he tells of this Indian buck who'd grown old. The ol' buck still gets around, but he can't hunt and so forth anymore. Well, one day this ol' buck just tells the Medicine Man that it's time for him to go on over to the spirit world. So the medicine man, he gets the tribe together, they dance and have this ceremony, sort of a party. The next day they build this rack, ya know one of those racks that's about six to seven feet off the ground, that they set fire to and cremate their dead? Anyhow, the tribe picks up camp and moves on, but not the ol' buck. He takes up his place on the rack and just lays down.

"Now the perfesser, he doesn't understand this. He says it's all superstitious savagery. He says this ol' buck just laid up there until he died. He says that's as dumb as a hurtin' dog bitin' its wounds until it kills itself.

So, my ol' friend, Bill, he sort of has had enough of this perfesser's bullshit, and he says, 'hey you schoolboy. You ain't got a clue what that ol' buck was about. With all your learnin', you ain't learned diddely shit. The only lesson in this here life worth learnin' is what life is about. You don't live life in your head. Life is about doin' and dyin'. When you can't do no more, it's just time to die. That ol' buck probably lived more each day than you have in your life time. You think livin's about bein' smart. You'd probably rather hang on in some dilapidated condition, maybe in one of them there fancy eastern hospitals, lettin' them doctors put needles and shit up your nose and out your ass. And I'll tell you why. You ain't learned to live and so you're afraid of dyin'! When you know what life is, smart fella', you'll know that there's a time to live and a time to die. Dyin' ain't so bad. Livin' is what's tough. Look at you. Your life could be rehearsed like some street play, in the mind of men. What do ya' think fella', ya' think that this head stuff can't be done when you're dead? When you die, you're goin' to leave that there body of yours behind. What the hell do ya' think ya' got it for?'

"Well, these two fellas didn't meet up again until after they did pass on over. And when they did, the perfessor says to ol' Bill, 'You know, that night in the bar when you jumped down my case, I want you to know that you changed my life. I took all my learning and started to feel with it. I discovered that all the reason and science in the world didn't fundamentally explain the miracle of life. I began to let myself just *be* instead of forcing myself to become something that I thought I *should be*. When the time came to die, it was easy. I had learned to live, and in just being me, I'd learned what I was and that led me straight to the Creator. I want you to know, I'm in your debt. It's amazing how just a simple truth can change one's life. By listening to you, my God became the Creator who molded me, the real me, not the me I was pretending to be. Up until then, my god was science, reason and so forth. Thank you Bill!'

"Now Bill, he paused for a long time, and then he said, 'Well maybe I should of listened to myself more. 'Cause when the time came for me to go, I'll tell ya' what, it scared the holy piss right out of me.'"

I thought about the story for a moment. "Are you trying to tell me that Bill didn't really have it together?"

"No guy, I'm tellin' ya' that life is just a little more complicated than livin' in the head or the heart alone. Ya' gotta, sort of, let it all be. Well ya' could just let it be, 'cause ya' gotta do nothin' unless you want to. If ya' use the ol' noggin to look at where ya' been, ya' can see where you're goin'. If ya' let the body tell ya' what it likes, ya' get an idea of becoming. If ya' allow yourself to think and feel fully alive and present now, ya' know what feeling is about. If ya' let the mind talk to ya' about what you're afraid of, ya' discover there's nothing to fear. When ya' live well enough to come close to dying, ya know you're alive. When the riddles lead ya' to laughing, you're gettin close to knowin' who you are. When living's a passion, you know who you are. You can't never be what you're not. Wisdom in your world, comes from knowing who you are and when you're in your own way and when you're makin' up the whole thing in your head. You are what makes you happy. And ya' can't run away from it and find yourself. God is about who you be. You can't find God somewhere else, boy. Ya' see he made ya', and his imprint is a part of who you are, and if ya' don't find that, ya' won't find nothin' in life worth living or dying for. You'll just kind of jerk yourself off to believing that ya' got some answer or something. Ya' just got to be, boy."

"I've got to be. What the hell does that mean? Like I'm not being now? Where does all this metaphysical mumbo-jumbo come from? *I've got to be.* That's like saying taxes are too high. It's just some sort of glittering generality that doesn't really say anything, like how you lower taxes and meet obligations. It's one of those fancy sayings that catches people up in false hope, confused thinking; hell, for that matter neurotic and psychotic behavior."

"Ya' know guy, I knew you'd say something like that. You've just spent too much time in people's heads, especially your own. All that schoolin' to be a psychologist has betrayed ya' boy. Can't ya' see that you have a pat answer for everything. I mean, if any ol' miracle came along, you'd explain it away as an illusion, a figment of imagination, a paranoid delusion, a rationalization, a fantasy formation and all that psycho-babble bullshit. Look, if ya' can't feel the difference between some head trip and who you really are, then you're so asleep that even I ain't gonna be able to wake your ass. Let me make it real simple. Ya' know what an orgasm is? Now when ya' go off, boy, do ya' think to yourself, this all could be some mental trip? That maybe it's not really happenin' or so forth? Well, I hope not kid, 'cause if ya' do, you ain't never known a real orgasm. Now when ya' do, there is this intensity, and it sort of overcomes thinkin'. Let's call it a moment of forgetting. For an instant, you're just alive with feelin'! And you forget **everything** else. Now that aliveness can be had in almost anything you do. But you tend to think of things like good and bad. So ol' Bill taught me that bad was good. Freezin' his ass off was so intense, that when he'd tell of it, you could hear a pin drop in that ol' bunk house. Now the perfesser, he didn't know before meetin' up with Bill, that livin' meant intensity. He thought, like you, that he could just think his way through life. Now ol' Bill, he didn't think much about thinkin'. So he could spin his yarns, but he never saw where he'd been in terms of where he was goin'. He didn't understand that feelin' so scared was nothin' to be scared of. He just sort of went from one kind of scared to the next, and when the end came, he met it scared. To Bill, life was about Bill, as if there was nothing when ya' die. Living and dying were just opposite sides of the same coin. Sooner or later it just happened. He never stopped to ask, and then what happens? Got it?"

I don't know if I had anything. Some of what Dink said made sense. Some of it seemed to just go in circles. I don't know if I even had accepted that some ghostly Dink was indeed speaking to me.

As I drove home I wondered whether or not I'd tell anyone, including my wife of this "conversation." I decided not to. I decided to write down my sunset chat with Dink and see what happened next.

Chapter Two

With intensity,
***being** is not a question;*
it's a passion!

Two days passed, and no Dink. During those two days I read everything I could get my hands on about channeling. No one writing about this phenomena reported what I had experienced. I questioned myself over and over again, had I just imagined the entire event—how could I tell what was real and what was the product of my own imagination?

And then the question, why *would* I imagine such a thing? Could there be some deep need tucked away in my subconscious that could only express itself this way? Had I repressed some part of me that was struggling to be recognized and integrated?

My research into channeling had revealed several theories to explain this phenomena. One theory asserted that the channeler was tapping into some other part of themselves, an alter ego. That made sense to me and was probably how I would have explained the matter without ever researching it. Not exactly a dual personality, definitely not true schizophrenia, but just a friendly chat with a part of oneself that normally hides from consciousness. Like day dream conversations—the kind we all had as children. Imaginary friends. And many channels openly admitted that their experience seemed like they were making it up at the time.

Another theory drew upon the holographic models of the universe set out by the Nobel-prize winning scientist, David Bohm. This theory argued that one mind somehow gained access to the whole holograph, and in so doing, the images became clearer. All things, indeed all knowledge, existed within the holographic nature of the universe, the one mind, and the individual mind somehow became attuned to this whole or another individual aspect of the whole, and amazing information followed. This theory could be used to explain people like Nostradamus and Edgar Cayce. Individuals who seemed to see through time. Perhaps this was indeed the source of revelation.

Still another theory insisted that the model of Rupert Sheldrake's morphogenic mind accounted for channeling and other so-called psychic abilities. According to this theory, there is a mind, or "M" field, and the individual participates in this field with or without their awareness. In fact, species participate in like fields within species and according to Sheldrake, this is why an acorn becomes an oak and not a rhinoceros. Further, according to this theory, a sort of Jungian collective mind was at work forming the reality of perception or expectation, at least for the human condition. Indeed, experiments have shown that this *mind field* accumulates according to the thoughts contributed. For example, one such experiment used a dedicated room and several groups of students to illustrate just this point. The groups were carefully selected so that they were even in terms of demographics and learning ability. When these groups were taught morse code, it was found that each successive group learned at an accelerating rate. In other words, group two did better than group one, group three did better than group two, group four did better than group three, and so on. The learning efforts of each group contributed to the ease of learning of the next group by somehow storing the collective mental efforts of each group in the *mind field* of this so-called dedicated room.

And finally, there were all sorts of theories about disembodied spirits that visited, haunted and even possessed the living. Maybe, I thought, that's what's really going on, I'm possessed. But if so, what happens next? Should I see a Priest and under go an exorcism or something?

"No guy, that won't help ya'. No Priest is going to solve your problem. You want to know why?"

Here he was again, the Dink, intruding upon my thoughts. "Yes, why?"

"Simply guy, you ain't got a problem. You have so lost yourself in all that theory that you don't even know a good thing when it bites your ass."

"I suppose you're the good thing?"

"Not exactly, but sort of. You see, you have all these false beliefs and they generate a very real false world for you to play in. Understand?"

"Hardly—a *real false* world. What kind of oxymoron is that?"

"An average one. But yes, you're living in an oxymoronic universe . . . it carries its own contradictions quite easily."

"Like thoughts are things, right?"

"That's a good place to start, but let's push it. Imagine a newfangled, synthetic computer experience; I think you call them virtual reality."

"Okay."

"Now, imagine that this virtual reality stuff was programmed by your thoughts. So, if you wanted an adventure, you got adventure. If it was romance you yearned for, you got so much lovin' you couldn't get it up afterwards. Got the picture?"

"Hard not to, but you're just a little rough around the edges aren't you?"

"Does that bother you guy? Do you think I should be more pious or something?"

"Well, I might take you more seriously if you were just a little more dignified."

"Yeah, but then you'd miss my point. Ya' see, you got this fancy expectation about spirituality. To you, to most folks, it's all about humility, dignity and reverence. Where's the laughter, the joy, the celebration in all that non-sense? Imagine that your Daddy gives you the greatest present in the world and says go out there son and have fun with it. What would you do? Kneel down and pray for further instructions? Or would you take that toy or whatever and go have a blast with it? Well God gave you everything you need, but he's not going to put it in for you—you gotta push. Hell boy, and I don't mean that literally, but you've been given this great gift of life! Don't take the damn thing so seriously; and that's just a figure of speech guy."

"You mean 'hell' is a figure of speech or life is a figure of speech?"

"Actually, both. The Lord spoke everything into creation, didn't He?"

"How am I supposed to know that?"

"Dontcha remember reading all those books like Genesis and the Rig Veda? You call them 'creation epics'. Don't forget, all the stuff in that there mind of yours is now known to me."

"Then why don't you clean up your grammar somewhat and let's have some dialogue that's both intelligent and educated."

"Oh, prithee, forsooth. Doth mine speech offend thine ears? Are thy sensibilities battered by my brute tongue?—Well bite me. You are so afraid of being **you** that it's not even possible for you to imagine, let alone comprehend, a life full of such intensity that considerations of being are no longer questions. Let your intellect ponder this: if reason is ultimately so final in its value or virtue, then what is *confusion*? Let me show you a circularity, a tautology as you would say. Reason exists to choose between alternatives. Multiple alternatives are another way of experiencing confusion. When there is no confusion, there are no alternatives, therefore no purpose to reason. One of the men you admire, Krishnamurti, said it this way, "One chooses only when they are confused." In clarity, there is no choice. And, my friend, I would add, choosing is an act of will. Clarity is an example of being. The only choice there really is, is simply to be."

I was a little taken back. Dink had come straight at me in a manner that did get my attention, and I must admit, some respect. "What then Dink," and as I said his name it felt good because it seemed like the kind of disarming familiarity I'd use with a friend just before I took them down a peg. "I mean **DINK**, what then is being?"

"Damn your dense hide, fella. It's simply this: What you are naturally is who you are. Whatever you do that is passionate to you, is who you be! For some, this is layin' on a hill, tendin' sheep; and for others, it's looking through a telescope at the stars. Don't you understand. Each of us is an aspect of Divine Creation. God experiences each of us that way. In this manner, we can give back to God His gift. Do you think you do God any great favors by pretending to be something you're not by communicating in a pretend voice?"

"No, I don't think that at all. And what makes you so sure that I'm pretending?"

"It's kinda like this. You like to wear cowboy boots, don't ya'?"

"Yes—they're comfortable."

"Ya' know what else? They remind ya' of when you were young. Dreams of riding on the range like Roy Rogers. Chasing the bad guys, being the *Hero* up on the silver screen, right?"

I hadn't thought of that before, at least consciously, but Dink was right. Cowboy boots were a sublimated Hero quest. "I suppose so."

"Okay now, let's imagine that you're goin' to give one of them there fancy speeches. Are ya' gonna wear those old brown boots?"

"They wouldn't be appropriate."

"Why?"

"Because they're not. They don't match a formal tuxedo."

"They ain't the problem, you are. You're afraid that ya' may not be taken seriously. You're afraid that ya' might be ridiculed. Wearing them there boots could be humiliating, right?"

"Possibly."

"Okay, now you're up there, in your fancy threads with those expensive Italian shoes. Ya' got a seventy-five dolla' tie on, right?"

"Go on."

"How does it feel? Is that tie comfy? How does your body like all that dress under them there lights on the stage? Sweat a little, do ya?"

"Sometimes."

"Yeah, and the truth is, ya' hate ties, don't ya'?"

"So what?"

"Simple, again, it's all so simple guy. You're afraid of being who you are. You've let everyone else tell you who you should be, how you should look, what's appropriate and all that there stuff."

"Are you suggesting that I maybe just go naked into the world, or something?"

"Does a bear shit in the woods, boy?"

"Why are you calling me boy and guy and fella?"

"'Cause it's who I am. That's my point, when I talk to ya' like ya' all wants me to, then ya' listen. But if I don't talk that certain way, then ya' tune me out; or at least, ya' try to. Now listen up, if you're gonna put that suit and tie on, have fun doin' it. What do you gain by hatin' it? If ya' cain't have fun, take it off and wear them ol' boots of yours. If passion ain't fun, it ain't passion! Got it?"

Chapter Three

The more you learn,
the less you know.
The less you think you know,
the more you are.

Who knows if I got anything? Dink seemed to be trying to tell me to be. Just **be**. And being was somehow natural and passionate. The question of **being** was suppose to disappear when one was **being**. I decided to try.

Dink was silent for the next few weeks. My schedule was hectic and each evening I fell into bed and almost without blinking fell sound asleep. My dreams seemed to be tutorial and often rehearsed long-forgotten memories. Each day I attempted to stay excited, full of passion about the moment, and surprisingly, I found myself more effective at my work and more at ease with myself. Even some of Dink's facetious and irreverent humor was slipping off my tongue from time to time. I actually found myself missing him.

My counselling practice was generally limited to successful people who in their own opinion had failed to self-actualize. Most of my clients were cerebral and lacked the emotional intensity Dink encouraged. But his ideas had precipitated an urge within me that I now freely shared with my clients. Don't misunderstand, I didn't tell anyone of the Dink—only some of his ideas.

One Wednesday afternoon, during a session with an attorney client, Dink suddenly interjected mid-speech, "and don't think all that thinking you mastered at law school is going to save your ass." My mouth formed these words before I could abridge them, almost like a parrot mimicking a master.

My client, Joe, looked startled. I must have too. We stared at each other for a moment. Finally, Joe spoke, "What?"

My thoughts raced. Now what was I supposed to say? My brain concocted several responses to Joe, but my mouth—previously so agile and glib—refused to utter a single word.

The Dink injected, "Easy Doc, just follow my lead. Tell him he's too damn cerebral—that's his problem."

With my mind still racing, I looked Joe straight in the eye. He appeared to be more disturbed than I had ever seen him. Joe had graduated valedictorian of his class. He was a well known trial attorney and he had turned down opportunities to sit on the bench. We had discussed his reasons and decided that, although his keen mind was perfect for meeting the demanding requirements inherent to being a judge, there was deep inside him a nagging low self-esteem problem that prevented him from trusting his own ability to judge. In fact, during past sessions I had actually encouraged him to accept yet another chance of a judicial appointment that had come to him. I had likewise encouraged his intellectual pursuits in a lot of areas including extensive readings in philosophy, psychology, and certain human potential books of the so-called new age genre. His readings had led him into serious studies of comparative religion and we had shared some delightful, non-billable hours just discussing the philosophy of religion and metaphysics. So now I am supposed to tell him he's too cerebral?

The silence only aggravated Joe. "How can you, of all people, say that I'm too cerebral? Where does that come from?"

"Joe, what I meant was that sometimes you lose sight of life by trying to experience it entirely in your head. I must admit that I am also guilty of this. For instance, last week when we discussed epistemology, how we know what we know, it was easy for us to ignore that the first fundamental of knowing is experience. To experience something our senses should be allowed to be fully alert and aware of the moment. A sort of passion results when we immerse ourselves in the depth of an event, mentally, emotionally, conceptually, as well as contextually."

"I'm missing something," Joe responded. "In fact, all that last dialogue sounds ambiguous, tautological, and extremely cerebral. For example, you chose four methods of experience—three of which seem to be purely mental in their nature. How did you put it? This passion which puts us in the moment—is achieved by mental, emotional, conceptual and contextual awareness? Would you like to tell me how that is different then the way I now experience myself or the world around me? Or perhaps, dear doctor, you'd like to define those mental epistemologies in some non-mental way?"

Joe's response was both concise and accurate. What a judge he would have made!

"Let me do the talkin' dear doctor," Dink said softly in my ear. "Make a note of that **Doc**, 'cause one day we'll discuss 'fixers'.

That's what a Doc is, ain't it?"

"Just get on with what it is that you want to say Dink," my thoughts responded, "and please say it in a manner that I can repeat."

"Tell him life is a process. The process is **the** only purpose behind knowing. Each of us has this ability, thinking, for the pure and simple purpose of being self aware. All the science and philosophy has no value unless they serve to enlighten each of us about ourselves. Use this analogy. Imagine a state of only consciousness, pure mind, if you will, and in this state all things are known and/or are calculable. Now, further imagine the study of anything, from pole vaulting to pool. You calculate force, trajectory, thrust, angle of approach, rotation, and so forth. Now let's assume that your calculations are all correct. That is, you "know" exactly what, when and how. Elaborate theorems, graphs, and so forth can be produced for any given situation in the games of pole vaulting or pool. Does this mean that you can pole vault, or that you are an expert in pool? The answer is an obvious and emphatic: **no!**"

As Dink's words entered my mind I spoke them aloud.

"So," we continued, "the world of shoes and ships and ceiling wax exists for learning. However, the learning is not mentation. Not that there is anything wrong with pure mental abstraction, for this too can be an expression of learning. Hell, for that matter, this type of thinking can, and for a few, often does approach such rhapsody that the process is both absolutely erotic and sensationally creative. It's pure and simple art in one of its finest forms. Still, the art form has no meaning until expressed in a medium. The idea of say, an image in the mind becoming the glory of a true work of art on canvas, is another example that can help us. The image in the mind is first not that simple to convey on canvas. Second, and most important, as the manifestation process begins, the image mutates—taking on a life of its own. As such, with works of art, whether a book, a poem, a painting, a sculpture, a musical composition or whatever, even the artist is unable to define precisely the outcome before it is completed. Indeed, as many creative geniuses over recorded history have reported, the process of creation is one of participation. As such, the creator is only a channel for the creation. The dimension of creativity associated with this level of God's glorious creations, is the precise process by which, and for which, the world exists."

"Where did God come from?" Joe interjected, annoyed.

Dink continued, or at least I continued to repeat Dink's words, "God is an expression. Choose a name that you are comfortable with. Call it a Muse, the Great Spirit, or anything, really. Just understand that there is a unifying principle in the world that orchestrates the very randomness and order which science observes and uses. Nevertheless, don't fall into that intellectual sciolism that purports to be in control of the world through their understanding of its "laws." For you see, these laws are really only observations of related events which once observed are believed to be understood. No such understanding yet prevails on this planet! Science is in the business of prediction, not control. When the prediction follows with events in concordance with the prediction, one easily falls into the deceptive belief that they are in control. Do you understand?"

Joe nodded affirmatively. He seemed deeply moved by Dink's comments and, I felt that I was about to glimpse something truly important myself.

"So, let's summarize our analogies. What you can do is all that you can ever truly say that you know. Why? Because doing imprints the learning at every level of your being. And even thinking has a doing characteristic, for when it becomes intensely enlightened, creative, the process is passionate—absolutely passionate. The entire being feels with the experience and it becomes an imprinted "knowing" just like riding a bicycle. Every cell of the being knows how to ride the bicycle because of the experience. Even twenty or thirty years later one can still ride a bike. Why? Because the learning level is imprinted by doing!"

Dink suddenly stopped speaking. The silence was finally broken by Joe, "Doc, that was the most meaningful session we've had. I know my time's up and I'll have to integrate the information for a while. Let's take it up again next week. Okay?"

"Sure. Same time next week," I said as I patted Joe on the back and accompanied him to the door.

CHAPTER FOUR

What you do
Is not who you be
Unless who you be
Is what you do.

"Hey guy," Dink rudely injected smack in the midst of some of my deep and profound thoughts, "Have you ever considered this? The universe is not a machine, it's a thought system."

"No—I can't say that I have. What is that suppose to mean?"

"Well, the universe is believed by most, including you dude, to be the product of laws comparable to how a machine works. Right?"

"Well, I suppose so."

"Now, guy, we've sort of got some things backwards here, so's now's a good time to get 'em straight. Ya' see, I've been given' ya' the answers and I'm here with ya' 'cause you're the one with all the answers. So, you tell me how the universe works. Just sort of think of me as one of them clients of yours, and council me on the great mysteries of life. Okay?"

"Council you! You want me to tell the all-wise Dink how to live and how to perceive the beauty and growth patterns of life? You're not even in life anymore—what on earth do you think I can tell you?"

"Doc, is that facetious? Come on now. Tell me what you think makes the world tick. Teach me from your perspective what life is about, who you are, or who any of us is and is about."

I hesitated. Not only did I have a Dink for a so-called channel, but instead of his providing me with answers and profound insights, he wished me to enlighten him. Interesting!

"Come on, now. Don't feel sorry for yourself. I know you would have liked maybe Asclepias himself to be your guide, if'n ya' had a guide. Right?"

"To tell you the truth Dink, I don't know. Some of your common sense stuff has appeal. But yes, probably. I imagine that given the choice, I would select someone like Buddha, Lao Tse, Zoroaster, or one of the great Greeks."

"Now I have a question? You're basically Christian. Why wouldn't you choose Jesus of Nazareth?"

Good question, I thought. "Probably because I see Christ in a position above that sort of thing. I mean, that's kinda of like channeling God."

"What would be wrong with that?"

"Well nothing is wrong with it. Do you know how many people believe that they do just that, and not only are they out on the proverbial limb, but they have sawed it off. I mean, take Jim Jones , for example. Do you think it was God talking to Jones?"

"Go on, Doc. I do like that Doc stuff."

"Well, all I'm trying to say is that demented minds create delusions and some of the most heinous acts of mankind have been committed in the name of God."

"Yeah?"

"Well, one must always check their motives. Operating within each and every one of us is this unconscious or subconscious process which strives to construct an ego identity that we are safe with. For some, safety comes through the security of power. For Jim Jones, power arose from his deluded idea that God spoke through him. However, since God spoke through him, to oppose Jones would have been equivalent to opposing God. It's a sort of mental self-aggrandizing which probably is the result of some deep-seated feeling of inadequacy."

"Okay, so what you're saying, Doc, is that the need for security may create imaginary means for generating security. Sort've a self-fulfillin' prophet, right?"

"You could say it that way. Three forces drive most people. Security, sensation and power. I mean, we have the four famous 'F's', fight, flight, feeding and well, the propagation of the species. These F's are built in, or hard wired as needs. These needs, or drives, fuel and direct behavior. But the whole process gets more complicated with man, as set apart from the rest of the animal world. Man uses cognition to interpret his world in a unique manner. We think about things. As a result, the four drives are often sublimated in order to meet higher social needs. Among other things, society creates morality. Therefore, in some cultures it is conceivable to give one's life for another, perhaps even a stranger, as a higher act of humanness. Still, society, at least our culture, has placed great value on security and sensation. Pleasure and pain are principles underlying sensation. All of us tend naturally to seek more pleasure and less pain, and that adds up to security and power, for power is really only a compensation means for obtaining additional security. They have become integral aspects of the pleasure side of our pleasure pain equation. People are, it seems, driven by the blind and total acquisition of security and power"

"I get it. So how does that make you feel, Doc?"

"Probably sad, more than anything else."

"Why's that?"

"I guess because deep inside me is the feeling that humanity has not begun to approach our potential. I believe that within each of us there rests a dormant giant. Free of the so-called normal bias. The giant does not re-act to the world but plays in it. The giant is not subtracted from, when someone else achieves a great success. Quite the contrary, the giant is increased. The giant is not jealous, avaricious, selfish and so forth. The giant celebrates the unlimited potential for expression that life offers. Power is a mere illusion to the giant, for power is truly of and within self. It is not something one has over another. That kind of power exists in the external world, but not in the internal. And it's not that power is necessarily bad, it's more that power is most often sought and used in the most devastating of power ways. In other words, it's kind of like, the more power for power's sake one obtains, the more that is needed because the more insecurity it actually breeds in the inner world of self. In fact, most people who obtain some power and then lose it are broken for precisely this reason."

"Go on. What about this sensation stuff you were talkin' about?"

"For most people sensation is as corruptive as power. The sensations most coveted by the world are immediate ones. Sometimes that's fear or terror. Probably the most successful forms of entertainment for the past several years have delivered fear; and if not fear, then sex. But I'm using fear in a special model. For fear and anger are opposite sides of the same coin to me. One becomes angry as a result of fear. And this type of fear is almost always the fear of loss. So our writers tell stories, and our producers make movies which portray some loss avenged in some manner or another, and along the way, some scintillating sex is thrown in."

"Is there something wrong with sex, guy?"

"No, it's not that there's anything wrong with sex. I'm not some puritanical celibate with righteous notions that condemn sex as a root of evil. It's that sex is not appreciated for the glorious event that it is."

"Sounds a little perverted, guy."

"You don't mean that, do you?"

"Well tell me what you mean by glorious event."

"Well, sex has the ability to take one to places that few other means can achieve. However, sex for power takes one to more sex for more power. Sex for sensation alone leads one back for more sensation alone. But when sex is an act of sharing, intimately caring, giving and taking, sensing and feeling for the joy of life, then it can become a transcendent experience. Still, my point is, it's rarely portrayed from its spiritual or metaphysical side. People would get uncomfortable facing this alternative to sex for sensation and power, and they wouldn't buy the book."

"So, let's see, sex is sacred? Sex is holy? Sex is spiritual?"

"Well yes and no. Those words can give rise to so much confusion."

"Seems like your world is full of confusion."

"Again, yes and no. The answer to that question entirely depends on to whom it is put. For some, there's nothing confusing about life. They have reduced themselves to purely stimulus and response, like animals they only know the drive and the method of fulfilling it. To these, the word life has no deep or resonant meaning. To philosophers, who think and are curious and who want to know why—as if they are driven by forces of spirit, not flesh—the meaning of life, the meaning of being, is all that really matters. And somewhere between these two extremes, is, I suppose some degree of confusion."

"Let me ask this, Doc, remember our conversation about confusion and choice?"

"It wasn't exactly a conversation, but I remember."

"Okay, if most people are confused about who they **be**, how can they be anything but what they do? Moreover, could it just be that the ultimate laws of the universe are such that to the precise degree one is confused, their world is confused? In other words, Doc, could it be that the world is a product of thought and the thinkin' itself produces confusion. A sort of chaos-and-order world, generated by disorganized thought from one level and consistent thought from another? And now, guy, I don't mean literally the chaos and order theories of physics, but the chaos and order which is humanity's history as well as everyman's story. Heaven and hell in the same moment for different people. For that matter, heaven and hell, pleasure and pain, from the same stimuli for different people. Think on this, we'll chat later, Doc."

"Now wait a minute, Dink!" but my plea went entirely unheeded. The dialogue ended. The Dink disappeared.

CHAPTER FIVE

What if the world we know
Is nothing more than what we know
And what we know is only if,
A tentative and transitory belief?

A universe of thought—not a mechanistic machine; or some of both, immersed without meaning, just thinking about thought. Those were the words I set down in my diary while my mind raced over the possibilities and ramifications. One thing I had always taken pride in was my willingness to consider all possibilities. What if complete paradigm shifts were only reflections of belief. This would mean that we all lived in a world of consensus, at least some collective unconscious consensus. That in turn would imply that each of our worlds were like overlapping points in time and space that appeared to coincide but indeed were uniquely different. Each of us would, for all intent and purposes, be experiencing our belief while another experienced theirs. And yet, the parallel nature of the events would be such that we would both agree on the general sameness of the event. Still, and more importantly, we could disagree on its meaning and experience. Although, we might even reach agreement about this by adding some caveat to our belief such as no two experiences are the same. Now we could disagree on what happened in terms of some subjective experience and still generally agree about objective matters. But do we even have to agree on objective matters?

As a scientist, my bias insists on objective agreement between reasonable people. But just what is objective agreement? Once again, I was forced back to consensus. An objective event occurs, the witnesses have an agreed upon criteria for validating, reporting and evaluating the event. This is precisely what science does. Is it possible, I pondered, that science is just another structure of thought creation which obtains its power by nature of the agreement between scientific minds?

"The ego is the creator of most things believed to be true, not the mind of scientists, guy," Dink's words interrupted.

"Dink, it sure would be nice if you'd knock."

"On your head?"

"No," I answered, peeved, "just—it would be nice if somehow you announced yourself and waited, if necessary, for me to complete what I'm working on or doing."

"Okay."

I began to become impatient when Dink went silent. "Look, you've already interrupted me. What are you going to confuse me with today?"

"Confuse you? How do you confuse the lost? I mean guy, you're lost. Don't ya' get it? Big time lost!"

"If I'm so lost, why do you bother with me?"

"That's it dude. That's the answer. You're so lost that I figure it won't hurt to mess with ya'."

"You have outstanding bed side manners. Are you here to assist me or attack me?"

"Neither. All I got for you is some thoughts that might move ya' off center."

"I think you've done that very effectively. What I want is balance, understanding, insight, wisdom, and **peace**."

"My last ma used to say, 'people in hell want ice water'. Wantin' comes in degrees. Ya' want understanding, insight and wisdom enough to give up what you already believe is true?"

"What do you mean?"

"Are you willing to give up everything to get nothing—no thing?"

"Is that suppose to be some sort of existential challenge?"

"No man, it sort of goes like this, there's a story about a young smart dude raised in a rich, powerful family. He decides one day that money and power are not enough. Ya' see, he's heard tales of this here ol' wise man that does miracles. So he sets out to meet this miracle maker and learn his tricks. You with me?"

"Yes."

"Okay, I'll call this young rich dude Cocky, 'cuz that's how he acts—at least in the beginnin'. So Cocky heads off to find Sage, and when he does, he sez, "Sage, I want you to teach me the secrets." Now he does this kinda like his rich daddy tells the maid to make the beds. So Sage looks at him and just walks away. Now this pisses Cocky off. So he yells to ol' Sage, "You know who I am?" But Sage just keeps on walkin'.

"Well, for a few years Cocky bad mouths Sage. He says ol' Sage is a fake, a quack and so on. But one day, Cocky, getting a little older and wiser, thinks again about Sage. 'Cause ya' see, one look in this ol' guy's eyes and ya' knew he knew something ya' didn't. So Cocky set out once again to find the ol' master. This time he takes just a handful of humility with him. When he finds Sage, he's down washin' his clothes by the river's edge.

"Well Cocky goes up to Sage and says, "Respectfully Sir, I really would like to learn the secrets of the universe. I truly wish to know the meaning of life. Will you please help me?"

"Now ol' Sage looks Cocky straight in the eye for a while and then suddenly grabs him by the back of the neck and shoves his head under water in that there river.

"Cocky fights to get loose but the ol' master's grip is too strong. Just when Cocky's about to start breathin' water, Sage pulls his head out. Now Cocky is spittin' water and gaspin' and so Sage takes him by the head, steadyin' his face so they are lookin' each other in the eye. The Sage says, "Tell me boy, while your head was under water, what did you desire most?"

"Cocky, not so cocky anymore, answered, "Why air, of course."

"Sage then spoke these words to the boy before leaving, "Desire to know as much as you desired air, and you will be ready to learn.""

I pondered for a moment what Dink was communicating in this

little story, and when I spoke, he was gone.

Desire to know. And yet everything I know is maybe false. Be willing to give up everything for no thing. Ego builds the world of knowledge. Is this to mean knowledge is false? What is illusion, what is real? As I locked my offices up for the evening, the questions racing through my mind portended yet another long and restless night.

CHAPTER SIX

What is real is eternal,
All else is inherently false.

"Dear Doctor, Sir. Do you have a moment?"

"Of course Mr. Dink," I responded, actually quite glad to have the Dink speak to me again. Weeks had passed. My schedule had been very busy but my mind was constantly churning both the words and the experience of **the Dink**.

"Would you like to know something—anything, and I really mean **know**. Not think you know, but to know in the sense that the knowing is undeniable? In fact, Doc, is there anything that you can say you know for absolute certainty?"

"Yes there is Dink. I hate to admit it, but I missed you."

"That assumes that there is a real you and a real me. Perhaps we're just characters in someone's dream."

"I don't think we are Dink, but I'm familiar with some of the philosophical thinking that started from similar premises."

"You don't think you're a dream, but what do you know? The question is, Doc, who are you?"

"That is indeed the question."

"No, Doc, that's the error."

"I don't understand—and please don't play mental gymnastics with me, I've had a tough week."

"Tough week? Ah poor Doctor, tell me what's wrong."

"There isn't much to tell Dink. It's just that these conversations, all the thinking, this whole matter has created some psychic tension. It's not so bad when I lose sleep because of our talking, but sometimes I'm way off in some other world when clients are here. I mean, sometimes I don't seem to hear a single word they're saying. That's a real problem. I don't feel like I'm doing my job. There are times I wish I'd never heard from you and other times I wonder where you've gone, actually wishing you were on call by demand."

"Is that what you'd like Doc? To have a Dink on call, by demand?"

"I don't know. Could we do that?"

"Maybe, if you're a good boy and get the point of today's stuff."

"I'm not sure that I've gotten anything up to now. How am I supposed to get the point today and how will I *know* it if I do?"

"That's precisely the point Doc, only a slight pun intended. Up to now we've been doin' this here mental masturbation stuff that you like so much. I mean, we've been all around this here head stuff and yet we haven't cleared anything up—have we?"

"Exactly what keeps me up nights.The answer is **no**. You haven't done much of anything except provoke me. It would be nice if you just told me the way it is. You know, some of that 'bear shits in the wood' philosophy of yours. Just give me the bottom line. I'd love it."

"Bet you would Doc, 'cause then you could just say either okay, or take a hike. At least that way, you could go on playin' with yourself. Right?"

"You think that's what I'd do?"

"No doubt about it. Hell man, you do it all the time. You judge everything. It's a good book or a dumb-shit author; good food or a lousy meal; good service or a lazy, minimum-wager; a good person or one screwed up bitch. And you know Doc, what you judge is according to what you agree with or like. Ever think of that?"

"What's your point? Aren't I just being? Isn't that natural Dink?"

"We've talked about natural Doc. What you mean is normal. And yeah, it's normal. But then normal is average and that's just the best of the worst and the worst of the best. Is average for you Doc?"

"Normal can mean more than average. It also designates an acceptable response, a reasonable attitude and so forth. So Dink, please, just tell me what you're here for."

"You."

After some two minutes, I spoke, "That's it. Me. You are here for me."

"Supposed to be something else?"

"How am I supposed to answer that?"

Like that poem you wrote, Doc, just last week. Let's see, how'd it go?

"Tell me, tell me,
Why is the sky so blue?
Or everything after a rain
Polished, glistening and new?

Tell me, tell me why,
Why do I seem to go through
Multi-dimensions of space and time
When I close my eyes—yet still view.

Tell me, tell me why,
Why are there only a few,
Genuinely concerned about
What can be said to be really true.

Tell me, tell me why,
Why is 'knowing' what I always knew?
'Be still,' the inner voice spoke silently,
'The **Y** in why is the first letter in **You**'."

"Did ya' mean that Doc? Did it happen, the inner voice and all? Or was that just some poetic bullshit?"

"Okay Dink—for me! You're here just for me. And to think that I was really looking forward to hearing you again. But for me, just for me, what pearls of great wisdom do you bring today?"

"You're just plain hostile to be around Doc. You must think I have to be here or somethin'. Maybe I should mirror some of you and tell ya' to get fucked."

"And how would this make you feel?"

"Now you're going to use that there psycho babble bull on me. How would I feel? Good, bad, judgements based on what, exactly?"

"Why would you suggest the behavior in the first place?"

"Give me a break Doc."

"Please explain. Elaborate."

"Give me the script. The next thing you're going to say is 'we were not talking about me. We were talking about you.' All this nonsense is straight out of your formula pattern for interviewing and counseling clients. So drop the shit. I said what I said because *you* felt animosity Doc. Remember, I read your thoughts and feelings. It's me Doc, the Dink. You're gettin' mighty upset with me today, right Doc?"

"You know, I do envy the way you use profanity sometimes. Because, right now, let me just say to the all-wise Mr. Dink, read my mind!"

"Good Doc, let it all out. All this confusion, all this suffering, all this pent-up anger, hey man, let it all out. You're feeling so sorry for yourself. You poor little picked-on shithead. And I know you resent me. The Dink—why couldn't you have some mighty Guru? Yeah, and you're right, how spiritual could he be with all this profanity? It's just your bad luck Doc to get me in the draw, not that there ever was a draw. I mean, let's be serious, how many ghosts do you think there are out there fighting over who gets to spend their earth time with the know-it-all Doctor? Hell, I could've linked with an astronaut and had a blast, but no, I volunteered for the arrogant, drowning shrink."

"I'm not arrogant. I have been very patient, all things considered. If you think that I am, then maybe you should go. Maybe there's a shuttle flight in your future and better luck in mine."

"Doc, that's the old ego talkin'. So was all them there nasty thoughts you was havin' just a minute ago. That ego is what I wanted to arouse today Doc, for the ego is inherently false. Let me say that another way, you have created your ego. You and mankind, culture, society, and so on, highly prize the individual and therefore the ego. God created you—not your ego. **YOU**. Just little ol' you. What God creates is eternal. What man has created that is not of God, is not eternal. Only the eternal is real. All else is false.

"Now I'm going to leave you here in a moment Doc, 'cause I want ya' to think on this for a piece. But before I go, remember what I said in the beginnin'. The question, 'what I be', is the error.

"Oh, and Doc, good luck and bad luck can be tricky to know the difference between. Just your bad luck 'could turn out to be just your good luck. Ya' know, there's this story told of an old rancher back in civil war days. Seems he was just barely gettin' by and all. His wife died havin' his only son and he was somewhat crippled up with arthritis. So his boy did most the work around the place. Now, our ol' guy was a real nice fella and everyone in town liked him.

"So one day, the boy's out tillin' the ground when lightnin' strikes near the mules. Well those mules just jump and bolt and the farmer's old harness cain't hold 'em—it breaks and they run off.

"Well, without those mules they can't get their crops in and they're barely makin' ends meet as it is. So the whole town turns out to commiserate. 'Such bad luck', they sez. But the ol farmer, he sez, 'good luck, bad luck, who knows?'

"Well, the next day those mules come runnin' home. And behind them comes a whole herd of wild horses. Hey, the farmer and his boy seize the opportunity ya' know, 'cause horses are worth a lot of money. I mean with the civil war and all, the armies on both sides are payin' bunches for horses. So they run out, open the corral gates, and when the horses and mules is inside, they close them there gates up.

"Well, the whole town comes out to congratulate, 'such good luck!' they sez But the old farmer, he just sez, 'good luck, bad luck, who knows?'

"Now, the next day the boy goes out to break them critters 'cause nobody is goin' to buy a horse they can't ride. Well, first thing, very first pony up, he just sort of switches over. I mean he goes up facin' west, sunfishes, and comes down facin' east, then rears completely over backwards. Hey man, the boy is lucky he ain't hurt more. A broken arm and collar bone, but the whole town comes out, 'such bad luck.' The old farmer, 'good luck, bad luck, who knows?'

"Now the very next day the army marches through town and they conscript every able-bodied man. Of course they don't take the farmer's boy, 'cause his arm and collar bone is broken. Okay, the whole town turns out again,'such good luck!' The ol' farmer, 'good luck, bad luck, who knows?'

"Now ya' see, that army was headed to Shilo. Not many lived. You just never know what's good luck and what's bad luck. But when your bones are broken, ya'll tend to think only of the pain, the inconvenience, the discomfort, and so on.

"So Doc, until next time, try to remember: Good luck, bad luck, who knows? On the other hand, the error in the question, 'what I be,' you should know."

CHAPTER SEVEN

Wouldn't it be just fun
if the trick of tricks,
when uncovered and done,
was that we tried to fix
a perfect ***SON****?*

It was late, or early, depending on one's perspective. Three in the morning and I was unable to sleep. Finally, I spoke aloud, "Dink, if you're around, I'd like to speak with you."

"Alright Doc, it's about time we took the next step. What's goin' on?"

"The error, the question, I haven't been able to work that out. Did you mean that or is it a riddle?"

"Oh, I meant it Doc. But are you sure you want to go into that now?"

"Yes, why not?"

"Well, I guess, since you can't sleep anyway, stirring your mind a little more won't do any harm. It's like this Doc, and I'm gonna tell ya' straight, without any pretense, ego is a projection created as a part of separation. Separation is a consequence of the original sin. When man decided to chomp on the fruit of the tree of knowledge, and that's a useful analogic, knowledge separated man from God. Not really, but in our mind, for knowledge is an artifact of our world. It's simply not wisdom and rarely is it empirical. By that Doc, I mean, the kind of radical empiricism William James offered, 'only pure experience is true'. So suddenly, man was inherently sinful, separated from the world of pure experience by our quest for the kind of knowledge that builds ego. Now, it's okay for us to play and have fun, and the world is kinda' our sand box, but we forgot it was a game we created. We lost ourselves in separation.

"You see, God created all things, large and small, just as the creation epics tell. When God created man, he gave us His ability to create. Good, except that we created this here separation.

"Now to **be**, Doc, ya' first gotta remember who ya' is. You was created perfect. You can never truly be out of God, no matter how hard you try, for you are eternal. You are therefore perfectly one with God, just as Jesus said, 'the Father and I are one.' However, man has this cute little function Freud called an ego. Now, the purpose of the ego is allegedly to protect you. But it's real purpose, is to protect itself. How about that Doc? An ego created by man to protect him that turns into a beast of survival whose first interest is to protect itself. Do you understand that?"

"Back up and go slow for me Dink—please."

"Awright, I'll say 'er slow this time. Ego exists to protect ego. Ergo, it's defense strategies are first separation. Us and them. The big ME as different from all else. It's tools are fear, shame, guilt and anger. When you are separate, you are alone. You are at the mercy of the world unless you have coping mechanisms and defense strategies to protect your being. Now this isn't your true being, rather it's your pretend being, or projection. Now there are two kinds of projection involved here, at least in the framework of our discussion. The first is projection of who you 'need' to be in order to be accepted. The second is projection onto the outside world as an inherently distrustful and separate environment. A bad place to be.

"Now, let me take a minute on this last bit. Ego projects onto the world an expectation. This expectation begins with the notion that you and the world are different, apart, separated. Now I'm not speaking here of so-called visible boundaries, but rather of essential, no, quintessential stuff. Some call this life force, others spirit, but I know you get the idea: A separation of spirit and matter.

"Are you sure you want to continue with this now Doc? It's going to get heavier."

"Yes! Absolutely!"

"Okay. But before I continue, let me suggest that tomorrow you go out and pick up a copy of the book, *Course In Miracles*. You see, what I'm gonna tell ya' is not new. No, in fact, I'll depart here and tell ya' a rather amusin' story.

"A few years ago there was this behavioral scientist working and teaching in a very conservative medical hospital. Well, things between her and this here associate, also a scientist, weren't goin' right. So one day, he sez to her, we've got to do something. There must be a better way for us to relate to each other, to work together. Got the picture Doc?"

"Yes."

"Okay, she agrees. Now what happens next is the unusual and amusing part of the story—but I promise ya' Doc, you'll relate. She's a jewish atheist and he's agnostic. But guess what? She starts channelin' this here information, wrote it down, and called it the *Course In Miracles*. Now, she's like you Doc, not too awful excited about what's happenin'. In fact, she even wonders whether or not she should go into therapy. Ya know—get help. Big time help. 'Cause guess what Doc, she's channelin' Jesus. Now if that isn't an irony. Now if she was like you, and I don't know Doc, 'cause I ain't met the lady yet, she'd be sayin' something like, "How come Jesus? Couldn't it have been Socrates or Moses? Give me an academic or a Jew". Right Doc?"

"Probably," I had to laugh. The Dink was right.

"Okay, and by the way, this lady is Dr. Helen Schucman and her partner is Dr. William Thetford, and this really happened at Columbia University Medical College. Now, as she takes down the notes given her, she discovers that the Course is all about who we are and what our relationship to everything is.

"So Doc, the next time we chat, it will be about the Course and its lessons. So again, please do us both a favor and pick one up. Okay?"

"Sure. But let's get back to what you were originally saying."

"Lemme hear you promise."

"I promise to read the *Course In Miracles* this week, if you will get back to the topic of separation."

"Yeah, but one more thing first. The beauty of truth is that it just **IS**! So all this material can be found in the sacred documents of the spiritual masters since the beginning.

"Awright, so the original sin, so to speak, was separation. Now the illusion of separation is perpetuated by the ego. The ego projects your fears, doubts, worries, and so forth onto the world. The world you see is what your ego expects. So, say you think someone is going to cheat you. They, or somebody similar in a similar situation, will indeed cheat you. And your ego sez, "See, what did I tell you!"

"You know, there's really only one mind in the universe. You are an aspect of that one mind. So is everyone else. In a very real sense, we all communicate with each other even if no spoken words are used. What's more, the laws of mind are not subject to the laws of physics. Rather, the laws of physics are subject to the laws of mind. In a minute, I'll give you an example, but first, let me make this point. Action at a distance is possible only because the action of mind is universal. Indeed, it is simultaneous.

"Now, the example. From about 1600 to 1750, there are repeated reports of persons either possessed or magnetized/hypnotized that levitated. Indeed, the psycho legal literature reveals that even those scientists who scoffed at some of the claims made by many involved in these areas, witnessed levitation. In fact, many of these conservative witnesses, and let's be realistic, many of these unfriendly witnesses, reported testing to insure that there were no hidden wires or tricks involved with the levitation. As such, the phenomena was known to be real. For a brief while, there were some who believed that a test for hypnosis was levitation. Now I am not kidding you Doc. You can find this information in your own library in one of those books you purchased for some reason, and yet have not read. The book is titled *Hypnosis, Will and Memory*. Do you remember it?"

"Yes. It's by Lawrence and Perry, isn't it?"

"It is. And as you know, their credentials are what you would term 'impeccable.' Right?"

"Yes. Yes they are."

"Okay, now maybe you might ask me, so what happened? Why don't folks levitate anymore? But since ya' didn't, let me tell ya' anyhow. What happened was simple. The collective belief changed. Ya' see, along about then came this here wise acre, Isaac Newton. He lived in that life time here on earth between 1642 and 1727. Now, Newton taught the world the basic laws of what you know as Newtonian physics. Among those laws Doc, is the rule, axiom, and we can add, belief, that objects heavier than air will fall to the ground. Voila! And ergo, no more levitation!"

"Dink, are you telling me that someone who believes differently will experience a different reality? And I don't mean just as a matter of the way they personally interpret the world, but as a matter of the actual physical laws that *govern* the world they inhabit?"

"You got it Doc! Let me just say it this way, 'cause I know how much Jesus of Nazareth has meant to you, do you think he walked on water? Don't answer. Next question, do you think you can walk on water?"

"No, I don't."

"Do you think you could ever walk on water if you did not believe that you could?"

"No. I guess not."

"So you already intuit, that to do something, anything, you must believe that you can, or at least, that it is possible. Right?"

"Yes, that makes sense."

"Okay, now Jesus asked, 'Why would you use my words and not do my deeds?' He also said, 'All that I do you can do and more.' He insisted that the Father has many mansions and that the kingdom of heaven is within. Are you familiar with all of this?"

"Yes, I am."

"He also said, 'I say to you, all things for which you pray and ask, believe that you have received them, and they shall be granted you.' You know this one, don't you Doc?"

"I do. Most certainly, I do."

"Now, did Jesus mean literally *all* things Doc?"

"I suppose so," but as I said this I became uncomfortable. I had never thought about this last question.

"Okay Doc, so if I want a pretty blond, I just believe her into my reality?"

I laughed and it immediately relieved my tension. "Dink, only you would ask such a thing."

"No Doc, indeed, many ask just this sort of thing without realizing what the consequences are. You see, you will create what you believe. Now get this Doc, cuz it's my one-liner for the night, **you are what you realize yourself to be!**

"So Doc, choose wisely what you wish to invest your beliefs in. The luxury of these negative, separating, punishing thoughts that most choose to believe, has a pretty big price tag. It's your choice Doc. I mean, the lesson, as they say in the *Course In Miracles*, is not optional, it's required; but the time you choose to learn it is entirely up to you.

"Now, another thing you should know Doc. The two most powerful creative forces in the world are fear and love. So, back to our little scenario where we expect to be cheated. This expectation is based on fear. Fear and limitation, but we'll get into all that there stuff in time. Still, Doc, this fear is a creative power. Man, I'll tell ya', watch those fears!

"Alright Doc, that's enough for tonight. I'm out of here. I've got work to do. I'm tryin' to talk all these damn angel folks into a rodeo in heaven. But ya' know, even up there we got some confused people."

"A rodeo," I inserted, "You're kidding me?"

"No, I ain't kiddin' ya Doc. Why? Does that bother ya'?"

"Yes, I guess it does. I mean, where do you get the animals? And there's some brutality in rodeos."

"True, at least here on earth. But ya' see Doc, that's one of the good things about heaven. The animals don't have to do shit unless they want to. And if you put on a rodeo, ya' gotto get the livestock to agree to it."

"Come on Dink, you don't expect me to believe that?"

"Sure. Animals are conscious. Hell, I wish I'd thought of that when I was down there on earth. Animals feel. They're part of the creation. They're involved in the evolution, or continual progression. Besides, anything I want, blondes and rodeos! But before you get too all-fired upset, consider this: ol' Mark Twain asks the question, and I'll just sort of paraphrase his thoughts. Ah, in fact, I'll just take a little license, and color it up some.

"Here you are, down on earth. Now ya' want to go to heaven. Most folks do. So I ask ya' why? What do ya' think there is in heaven for ya'? Typically, the answer is something like this, 'peace and tranquility.' You know Doc, all those ideas of harps playin', angels singing' and so on. But what a bore if it turns out that there's nothin' to do. 'Like that ol' sun, just rolling around heaven all day.' Like a hamster on a wheel, Yeah?"

"Go on, I'm not sure where you're going or what you mean."

"Figures. So ya want to go to this here heaven with harps and angels and nothin' to do. Now, most of ya' would hate it if that's what bein' here on earth was about. Why the hell, oops, excuse me Sir, I don't even like harp music—well, except for that pretty lady Georgia Kelly and the funny guy, Harpo. But my point is simple. Why would you sacrifice this life to obtain a heaven that has nothin' in it ya' would want or like while you're down here on earth?

"So remember that guy. Living is meant to be a joyous experience. You're not here to be punished. The only reason you don't know the peace that passeth understanding, or the joy that Jesus knew, is inside you boy; just as the peace itself is.

CHAPTER EIGHT

Fear is the absence of LOVE,
LOVE is living in gratitude.
Fear is inherently false,
LOVE is eternal and real.
The eternal cannot be threatened.

I did purchase a *Course In Miracles* the next day. I began reading between appointments that afternoon. The academic credentials of the two people involved in producing the Course were impressive. The Course made sense and seemed to reach resonant notes within my being. Still, some of its ideas together with the very manner in which the book supposedly was generated were just a little radical for me.

"Radical Doc?" Dink injected his words into the midst of my thoughts.

"Yes."

"Let's set radical aside for a moment and go back to where we began. We started with this idea of being, and just being who you is. Right?"

"Okay. How was the rodeo, by the way?"

"Later on that Doc. Gettin' on with bein', we might by now argue that **being**, being in the natural, just being at being, first requires that we get some clues as to what and who we is. Right?"

"We've already agreed on that."

"Well, if you say so. Now let's think about this, in the beginning God created man, and I don't mean that in the masculine sense only, 'cause it would be one dull world without them there females. Although, you know there really ain't neither—male or female. No, there ain't neither one and there's both at the same time. But that's another subject. So anyhow, God created you, me, us, all of us. Now we're perfect ideas in the mind of God. Remember, there's really only one mind, God's.

So you and I are created perfectly. Now what happens is this: We ask ourselves, what am I? Or, more personally, who am I? The moment we do this, we have created a boundary—ourselves as unique and distinct from the rest of the world of creation. Now this gets complicated Doc, but we'll use some analogies, maybe a story or two, and see if we can make it a little clearer.

"In the beginning, or what we'll refer to as the beginning if for no other reason than the limitation of linguistics, there was singularity. The primordial and proverbial Un-moved Mover, shall we say. Then, there was what your scientists term a big bang. In other words, God divided himself in creating man. Now the only thing that God created was man. This is important. God created only man. All other creations are the creations of man. Still, man can only create from the "stuff" that is God. In other words, all things are in the body of God.

"Okay, just as with the big bang, and for clarity, try to remember that I'm speaking in analogies and metaphors here. The real difficulty in discussing most metaphysical propositions is the limitation of language; or more precisely, the inability of the finite to comprehend the infinite, let alone describe what has not been comprehended. But, just as with the big bang, singularity became diversity. Now this diversity was and is intelligent. What's more, because it was made in God's image, this diversity was invested with the ability to co-create which itself is sameness.

"Awright, imagine that the primordial stuff was a highly compressed form of "something." So compressed that it did not take form as we know it; that is, it was not liquid, gas, solid etc. Indeed, so compressed that even the notion of fields is inappropriate. Now, this primordial "whatever," suddenly expands into what we could call the seas of the universe. From singularity, as your great physicist Stephen W. Hawking calls it, all things are born.

"Now the universe has separated from its origin and flies out forming all sorts of "stuff" we call electromagnetism, gravity, material or matter, energy, macroscopic to microscopic and fields and forms not yet known. As this universe goes out into the nothing, filling the void, its relationships with other parts of what was the same gives rise to producing relational positions, and that produces time.

"Take your paper and pencil and look at it for a moment. All things and no things are to be represented in a single dot. Mark that dot on the paper. Okay, now before we go on, understand that a more accurate model would be absent a dot, absent the paper, absent you and me, but this is not a model that will communicate what I'm attempting to share with you.

"So, in that one dot on your paper, imagine that the dot is all there is. Only the dot. No paper and so forth. Okay Doc?"

"Yes, okay."

"Alright, now from the perspective of the dot, is there such a thing as space?"

"No, there couldn't be, because there is only the dot. Well unless, the dot is large enough to have space within its boundaries."

"Leave it to you Doc, assume that the dot is so homogenous as to have no such thing as what we would call shape and so forth, and therefore no interior or exterior or boundaries. All there is this damn dot. Okay?"

"Okay."

"Awright, now draw one more dot anywhere on the page. That's good, now connect the dots. What you now have is a straight line. Right?"

"Right, but if the first dot represents both everything **and** nothing . . . then what does the second dot and the line represent?"

"The second dot is the reflection of the first dot. A mirror image that, when sufficiently reflected is but one reflection or aspect of the initial one dot. The line is both the distance and the time for as consciousness reflects upon itself it enters the domain of time, which is distributed in the universe as space. They should not be seen separately for that is not possible. The line then is *time space.*"

"Alright. I think I understand that. Einstein essentially argued for time space as a single unit."

"Okay, now add a third dot and then connect it so that all three are interconnected. What has been created is dimensional geometry. In the line, assume the dots to be erased, there is only a line. The line is continuous and therefore a part of itself. As such, separation is not present until the line curves back on itself—to create dimensional geometry. Only in separation is there such a thing as space. From space is born the differing positions from which observations of what your scientists call light can be made as light passes by. Imagine yourself contemplating yourself. As you contemplate yourself, there are so many aspects of your being that each aspect can be represented by a dot. Now, give each dot, or aspect of yourself, the ability to look back and recognize itself as distinct. This is the illusion of separation. Separation has therefore created both time and space, or at least what more appropriately is the illusion of time and space. Are you with me Doc?"

"I think so. Please continue."

"Awright, now as with the big bang, in the beginning there was only God—the Big Singularity—just like most of the creation epics say. God divided himself creating man. Man, as a co-creator, created all else. These creations are a part of God and respected by God for they were created by the Son of God. God's gift of creation was unconditional and therefore we can create as we so choose, and believe me, so we do; although for the most part we are ignorant that we have a choice in the transaction. However, at the same time, the creations of man are not real for they are not the creations of God. God's creations are of himself, so to speak, and therefore perfect. Perfect in this sense clearly also entails eternal. What is eternal is real. All else is inherently false. It is a part of the illusion created by man.

"It's kinda like that holographic world we talked about. Man's role in the holograph provides for his ability to select the characteristics inherent to the whole, and organize them as he sees fit—usually just as a matter of expectation and belief, both singularly and collectively.

"Now most creation stories differ some here, as you know. You see, there have been classically three ways to interpret the world and how it came into being. The first is as the creation of God and thus all those fancy teleological, cosmological, cosmogony and so forth arguments for the world, as evidence of divine architecture and therefore a proof for God. Another perspective has been that of natural selection, natural order, nature herself as a non-entity with special entity status that set up all these rules of survival, evolution, and so forth. This argument, to me, is so essentially flawed that no one sees its error. If, for example, nature designed all of this stuff, set the rules in place, and so forth, then haven't we just renamed God as an intelligent, designing force rather than an entity? So the third interpretation comes into play, and that is the entire thing, the whole of the universe, is just an accident. It just happened. There is no sufficient cause. Cause is unnecessary even if it leaves each of us empty—no cause!

"Now, indeed what occurred is no more nor less communicable than the big bang theory itself. From singularity, God, to separation, man, all manner of known and unknown came into the world of illusion, what the Asians call maya, what we tend to call reality. Alas, the world of shoes and ships and ceiling wax is born. However, just as with the big bang, sufficient cause is implied. And just as with the big bang, the collapse of all things back into this primordial singularity is certain. The schedule is the only tentative matter. And because there is no such thing as time—this collapse back into a unified God has happened—is happening—and will continue to happen. You get to choose.

"Thus, I told you the lessons are not optional, only the time taken to master them is elective. Just as the expanding universe will at some point stop expanding and begin its slow, inevitable collapse upon itself into one inconceivably huge gravity point, so the individuality of the separated ego will surrender the illusion and return to its singularity, God.

"Then **being** natural first requires remembering who you **be**. You **be** a perfect creation of God, and you are never out of that **being**, even if you pretend to be. And we'll discuss this at great length sometime in the future—which as I said, also doesn't really exist. But to **be** is to **be** entirely in the moment. When this truly occurs, time is non-existent. Thoughts, as you know them, do not occur. In that precious moment of eternal **now**, being who you **be** is at-one-ment, or what Christians have compressed into an *atonement*.

"Any other form of being is an illusion created by man. Indeed, it is a projection of his ego onto the world. This projection serves the purpose of preserving the ego by insisting on separateness.

"Now, so you don't misunderstand, the creations of man are respected by God. Man and his world are **not** inherently evil, even if they are false, or dreams within dreams. You are entitled to have as much fun as you wish with your creations. And there is the real irony. You have the ability to create for the very reason that it provides you creative fun and unique adventures in experience. It's sort of like being given the power and ability to generate your dreams according to whatever you desire. But, do most create fun? Unfortunately, there are many who choose to create nightmares, like being addicted to horror films. The only thing that will entertain them, fulfill their expectation, are dramas with horrific implications and endings.

"Take sickness, for example. Sickness is a matter of sin. The only sin is separation. Sickness exists in man's mind. It serves to punish him, to attract or gain attention, to avoid and/or to deal with unresolved conflict which is producing psychic tension. In short, the creation of man called sickness, is one of his ways out of the perceived reality which the ego insists is independent and separate. But again, we'll discuss this more in that non-existent future that I mentioned in the non-existent past..

"Okay Doc, all this philosophical intrigue, together with its epistomological swerving, has tired this ol' cowboy's synapses. It's time for me to get on out of here and let you ruminate."

"Wait Dink, or actually Mr. Dingle, that somehow seems more appropriate now. Please wait."

"Doc—please don't call me Mr. Dingle. I'm just ol' Dink. And I don't want to be otherwise."

"Alright, but I have some questions."

"Knowed you would. I'll play genie and give you two. Choose them carefully. Okay, what's number one?"

"How can you go through all of that difficult and challenging information and turn around and talk like some unlearned hick?"

"That's one Doc."

"No, no, no. That's not one of my questions."

"Well you asked it, so it is now. And here's the answer. Don't take yourself too seriously. Life is not meant to be difficult. This is your playground. Have fun. Do it with respect knowing that God is in all. Treat all as if the God center in all mattered, or just as though you were dealing with God. But Guy, do it with fun and joy! You don't have to be all dead serious about spirituality. The presence of that moment in now teaches each of us that joy, love, happiness, just good ol' fun feelin's is what now **is.** So I'm tellin' ya' guy, lighten up. Stop and smell the roses. I mean, enjoy this world, that body, this life. Do as Jesus admonished, become a daisy in the field or a lily in the river or whatever. Use this experience you call life to its highest and best good. Give, share, embrace—hell man, oops, excuse me again Sir, heaven man, walk in gratitude, and LOVE is all that you'll know."

"Gratitude—that's it?"

"That's question two Doc, and I'll bet that keen mind of yours did not intend to use your two questions as you did. Nevertheless, here's your answer."

"Wait Dink, that's not fair."

"Bad luck, good luck—who knows? Well here's your answer anyhow. Gratitude is the absence of fear. One cannot be grateful, truly grateful for all and everything, and have even the tiniest remnant of fear remaining. Elsewise, what happens is a fella says I'm feeling good and grateful today and that ol' subconscious, that ego, says, maybe, but remember you could have this or that happen any minute. Or it begins to remind you of controversy and conflict and suddenly the ol' mind has shifted into that familiar fear place. In fear the ego is safe. Why? 'Cause ya' think you need it. You see, the ego needs you to need it. You know, some of that heuristic jargon you lay on clients, like co-dependence. The first co-dependent relationship was between you and ego. The two are as abusive to each other as any other co-dependent role. In fact, more so. You see, the ego is a truly abusive fella. When you realize that only ego stands between you and God's realization in you now, then you will get a grip on just what a nasty ol' sucker this dude is. But until then, you might just listen to ol' ego raise up his head now with thoughts like, this is so much bullshit. The world is obviously more than a dream and I ought to hit ol' Dink in the mouth so he'd remember the pain. Ya' see, pain tells you the world is real. And Doc, there are all kinds of pain, as you know.

"So there's yer answers Doc. Remember now, as ol' ego works on all this here material, keep readin' that Course and let your feelings carry as much as your head. Ya' see, all these here words are only approximations, which experience alone can know. Language is inherently incapable of communicating some things. Models such as our big bang stuff can help. Allegories and metaphors are helpful too. But in the bottom analysis, what matters is that *knowing* experience. So let yourself feel these thoughts while that cortex percolates. Okay?"

"Okay. But Dink, one last thing please."

The Dink was gone and for the first time, I felt foolish even thinking of him as the DINK.

CHAPTER NINE

Oh what a web we weave
In "laws" of the self-deceived.

"Hey Doc. Wake up Doc."

"Dink? Is that you?"

"Mmf," my wife said, stirring from sleep. "You say something?"

"Yeah. It's Dink," I whispered. "Go back to sleep."

"Mmf . . . "

"Get out of bed Doc."

I lifted my head from the pillow and set my feet on the ground. The Dink had never awakened me before and I sensed that there was something very important. I tried to hurry.

"Okay Doc, we've got some things to hash over. Are you ready?"

I sat down at my desk and nodded my head.

"You know the missus is pregnant?"

"What?" my startled answer echoed off the glass doors of the china closet and seemed loud enough to wake the dead.

"Easy Doc, you guys been wantin' a little one for a piece now. Well, guess what? Ya' got your desserts a cookin' in the ol' oven."

"Are you sure Dink?"

"Yeah, I'm all too certain!"

"Well, is it a boy or a girl?"

"There's considerable argument over that right now Doc. But you and I got other matters to take up, and we're gonna have to accelerate this here information exchange now that Momma's about to make ya' a daddy."

"I don't get it Dink. Why?"

"Well, we'll discuss that another time. But for now, let's get back to this here world ya'll like to think is so real."

"Dink, I need a cup of coffee first. Let me put some on before we start, okay?"

"Go ahead Doc, I understand. Boy did I used to like my first cup of coffee in the mornin'. A cup of coffee and a good smoke, man that is how to start the day. They're not just for breakfast anymore."

"I don't know about the smoke Dink. That stuff will kill you."

"Oh Doc, that's nonsense. Well, maybe it's not, but it sure won't unless you believe that it will."

I had made my way to the kitchen while the Dink continued.

"Ya' know Doc, Jesus said, it isn't what ya' put in your mouth, but what comes out of your mouth that will get ya'. And, if ya' think about it, Buddha was a fat ol' dude, so you'd probably put him on one of them there microbiotic diets you been thinkin' of for yourself."

"Dink, we have a lot of studies that show clearly the damaging influence tobacco has on the human condition. And Jesus was clearly implying the dangers of second-hand smoke when he warned about what comes out of your mouth."

"Funny guy. Yeah—you got lots of studies carried out with doses no hundred chain smokers would ever accumulate in a life time, and lots of studies done by guys who knew the outcome in advance and co-created it, and lots more studies that show anything and everything is a so-called carcinogen. Plus Doc, all those smokin' studies show something else that most don't get told. They indicate that personality determines the effect of smokin' on the body. You know that Doc, that's suppose to be one of your specialties. You know that the guy who internalizes his emotion and smokes, gets cancer; while the guy who is openly hostile and aggressive, gets cardiac disease. So come on Doc, recognize at least that the person's personality, which is a kin to his belief system, is as much, if not more of a factor in health, than anything else."

"Your point is well taken Dink and it explains why some people drink poison and handle snakes in church and get bit, and come out fine. But it doesn't matter, you don't smoke anymore."

"Who says. Hey guy, remember—**anything**! Well maybe my blonde is a good ol' cup of coffee and a smoke."

"Yeah, and maybe God is a blonde?"

"Good point Doc. Have you ever considered that before?"

"What exactly."

"God as a babe."

"I can't say that I have."

"Well, let's just chase that there idea for a moment, 'cause it will help us get to the stuff I wanta talk to ya' about tonight."

I sat back down at my desk with my coffee and took the first sip. Dink was right, that first cup of coffee in the morning did hold a special pleasure in it.

"Alright Dink, go ahead and chase. I'm ready."

"Well Doc, let's back up first and think about how most folks think of God. He's a dude first, right?"

"I suppose," I couldn't help but laugh at Dink's use of dude in this context.

"Okay, now this male god is the old anthropomorphic God of Moses, for most. Just the way Michaelangelo painted 'im on the Sistene Chapel—white hair—long white beard—not a teenager with acne. Right?"

Again Dink's imagery took me off guard, only this time I had to choke down some coffee as I laughed. "No, I don't think so Dink."

"No indeed. Can ya' imagine even thinkin' that way? Huh?"

I chuckled but did not answer.

"Alright Doc, for most, God is this wise old man, wearing a robe and sandals, that sorta sits around on a throne in heaven. And that's it. I mean, he can be pretty stern, but mostly he's just a lovin' god. That just sits there—never eating or brushing his teeth or even changing clothes. Right?"

"The way you say all of this seems somewhat blasphemous Dink, but I do agree. For most people in our society, God is a man that is wise, strong, good and powerful, who just sits there watching and judging."

"Ya, that's it. All of them things plus some. Now think of this, God is to a woman maybe the ultimate masculine image. Yeah?"

"That's interesting Dink. Go on."

"Well, you've heard of them nuns and sisters who believe God comes into their bodies and makes love to them. Hell—oops—Heavens! They even have orgasms. Right?"

A patient of mine who claimed to have just this sort of experience immediately flashed into my mind. "Yes Dink, some claim to have experiences of this nature."

"Well Doc, do you think they're makin' it up?"

"Yes. Most certainly. It's a product of the imagination."

"Really Doc. What is a wet dream?"

"Same as the other, I guess," again I found my self chuckling.

"Is it any wonder Doc that so many cute young gals go for some of these older gents?"

"I had not made that connection before."

"Well now stop and think about it. Do it this way, imagine God as a woman. What she look like? I mean, is she buck-toothed and cross-eyed? No man, the most beautiful woman you can imagine is what she'd look like. And add this bit in to your thinkin' Doc: she'd not be ashamed like in the garden of Eden. So there wouldn't be no clothes on her either. Now Doc, ya' come face to face with her, I mean real close, what's goin' on in your head when this happens? And what about the bod? Ya' gonna be tryin' to think of something else to control old homo-erectus or will he just stand up and salute?"

Dink's words were both funny and blasphemous, once again. "Am I going to feel guilty for laughing at these one-liners in the morning Dink?"

"Should ya' Doc?"

"I don't know. That's why I'm asking."

"Let's look at it a little different. If you really want to know something about heaven and God, wouldn't you ask all of these questions, unless you felt too much guilt and inhibition to even think about askin' 'em? I mean, it's okay to ask about hell and ol' Lucifer, ain't it?"

"I understand what you are saying Dink. It's just that some things are sacrilegious."

"Who told you that—and why did ya' believe them? Ah, never mind, let me just go on here for a minute. My point is simple, heaven and God are not what most folks think they are. In fact, they aren't separate—they is an it and it ain't a thing at all; well, and I suppose it is, but them there words don't make it possible for me to be all so clear here. So suffice it that heaven, God, hell and the devil aren't what they's thought to be. In other words, let's get at what they are by speaking first about what they're not. Okay?"

"I'm with you, I think."

"Alright, now we've talked about God and heaven enough for the moment. Let's take on old hell and it's oven master. Hell is in the minds of men. No where else, except as man creates it. The ol' oven master, that's man's separation, his ego. You want the punisher, look at the ego. This damn ego has to convince you of your separateness from God in order to exist. The war in heaven is inside you guy! When you accept that you are less than what God created, mortal and frail and sinful and so on, you've just given your power to the oven master—your ego. Now, and only now, can ego punish and control you. Ego will serve you up with massive doses of guilt, fear, jealousy, envy, avariciousness, anger and so on. Ego will fool you into yesterday's guilt and the fear of tomorrow. All of this is to defend you from a hostile environment; maybe even a hostile god. But it's a big, fat LIE.

"You see, God is LOVE, only love, unconditional love, but ego would have you believe that God is capable of being vengeful and wrathful. The reason you believe this, is because the holy spirit, the god remnant in us all, nudges you to remember the separation. That nudging produces, at an unconscious level, becomes the feeling of guilt. Guilt for separating, but ego raises it's snake-like head with defenses. So these here mechanisms you call projection, repression, sublimation and so on, protect the ego—**not you**!

Now think Doc, use that there Ph.D. for something other than **P**ilin' it **H**igher and **D**eeper. Think. The ego, and here I don't mean ego generally as the dynamic other apart from the self within you. The self you know is capable of more. Rather, I speak of the ego that says it's okay, you'll do better next time, or it's okay, the son-of-a-gun deserved it. That ego, not the so-called total psychoanalytic ego of super ego, id, and so on, but one ego. That ego is not who you are and you know it. Plus Doc, the self that is not your higher self is not you either. But ego, and this other projected self, the self you think you should be, these two have this here truly co-dependent relationship. To exist, they need each other. Who pays this price Doc? You.

So, Doc, think about this until we talk again. The ego is not real. Only the eternal is real. You, the real you, is real. That real, eternal you is in God. It is as pure today as it was in creation. The chasm between these different parts of you, ego, projection of self, higher self and more, many more for some folks, this is not only the stuff of pathologies, as you call it, but the stuff of true self-alienation. Accept that God lives in you now, is you, all that you can ever be is God's gift to you, and life changes Doc. Get this lesson well into that head of yours. Ego is not real. Fight it, and you give it power because you acknowledge that you must fight it. Love it away, it has no power. Love is the certain path to higher consciousness simply because it cancels ego's grip on you. Ego only works if you can get angry, be fearful, feel guilt and so on. Allow the Christ consciousness to be who and what you are and you **be** what you are!"

With that, the Dink was gone.

CHAPTER TEN

Roses are red,
Violets are blue,
The trickster is Dink,
But so are you.

Several days had passed since Dink awakened me in the mid of night. I had followed his instruction and read daily from the *Course In Miracles.* The material Dink had given me made the Course seem very familiar, or did it. Somehow, a part of me sensed that at some level of my being, I already knew the lessons and instructions given in the Course. I decided to try calling on Dink for some additional insight.

"Dink, are you there." There was no answer, so this time instead of thinking the question, I stated it aloud, "Dink, are you there?" Still, no answer. I shrugged and spoke half out loud, "You're never there when I want you."

"Really Doc," Dink answered. "I think I do a good job of waitin' on you to be ready for me."

"Waiting on me?"

"Yeah Doc, you can be kinda slow about processin' all this stuff, and that worries me."

"Why?"

"That's another subject Doc, but how's momma doin'?"

"Fine, and she thinks you're right. She's going to pick up a home pregnancy test today. She says she feels pregnant."

"Sure she does Doc. But let's get on with what you called for. What can I do for you today dear Doctor Sir?"

"Dink, this whole thing about heaven and hell is a little clearer to me, but there are some ambiguities that I'm struggling with."

"Like what, for instance?"

"First, if man creates everything except himself and God, how did we stray so far from Source?"

"The how is not what you mean. What you seek is the why. Why would man leave that proverbial garden of Eden to enter a world of confusion, conflict and scarcity? That's what you really want to know, ain't it Doc?"

"Yes, that's correct."

"That ain't such an easy question to answer, but here goes. In the beginning, and every day since then, man has questioned, 'What am I?' We've been all through that. But, inherent in the question is the confusion. I mean, why would a person be asking such a silly question in the first place? Right?"

"I don't have the answer, but right, why have so many asked that question?"

"You see God gave man knowledge of individual self as well as co-creative power. Now to create necessitated consciousness, or what some call awareness. So each and every aspect of God's creation was given awareness. Now this can be a little confusing, so let's use a model or two and maybe some metaphors. Remember those drops of water we discussed?"

"Yes."

"Okay, let's say that each drop of water in our metaphor is given awareness. It is a unique creation and yet it is not. Understand? I mean, collectively the drop of water is a part of the entire sea. Got it?"

"I think so."

"Still, each drop is aware. Now collectively aware is truly aware. But then, there is also uniquely aware. When one is both collectively and uniquely aware, they experience the **at-one-ment**. But, at the moment of awareness man begins to create. The product of this creation is what gives rise to asking, 'What am I' for the sake of identifying our creation. This may sound a little strange, but think of how you create now. Remember that your thoughts are creations even if insufficiently intense to manifest in the world you term 'reality'. What happens within you when you create what you perceive as an original thought?

"Think about Albert Einstein for a moment. According to him, while resting one day on the side of a sunny hill, he began to imagine that he was a beam of light going out into space. As he traveled near the sun his light beam began to curve. Well, according to Einstein, it took him the next twenty years to convert this "imaginary" experience into what you now know as Einsteinian physics, the curvature of space, time, $E=MC^2$,

Relativity, and so forth. All of this was the product of a moment in imagination. But now, here we're getting to the point. While in the world of imagination where there was no **self** per se, the curvature had existed since time and space began, in the one mind. However, as soon as this curvature was *perceived* at that level of uniquely aware individual awareness, known now as Einstein, then it was manifested into his consciousness as a novelty of his creation or an idea. This consciousness of the novelty led Einstein back to individual self. Just as an awareness of novelty led man to individual self and/or the questions: 'What am I?' and 'Who might I be?'

"Now Doc, again remember that for our purposes we use models. This explanation is but a model or metaphor designed only to assist you in understanding my response to your question. Still, I would be remiss if I didn't point out to you that your original question, as usual, is entirely irrelevant. But now the model gets even deeper. I'll elaborate on it now, and then maybe later we'll chat some about it.

"In the ONENESS of God, our sea in the last metaphor, there is no question, no teaching, no learning and so forth. That's because everything is known. As such, answers to questions that arise only as a result of the illusion are moot. The question is a mental calisthenic relevant only in a world of definitions such as this. The answer is only a mental tool designed to facilitate the exercise by removing ego's ability to marshall some argument of logic as a defense. For, if ego discovers that you see that it is playing a game, which you choose no longer to play, it will first attempt to frighten you from leaving the game and next attempt to maneuver you into believing that you are playing the game as to pretend not to be playing at playing. If it were not for this damn ego shit, I could just tell you that the question of who you are is about as relevant as what did God do before he did anything. You see, this is only a tautology. The inherent circularity in the question makes any answer either contradictory or recursive. Your philosophers often miss this nonsense. Some of them even attempt to pretend that language had some 'real' meaning or value independent of observation or experience. Whatever you do with language, remember that it is at best only an attempt to describe. At worst, it is the tool of lies. Think about that Doc, for without language there exists no lie. Now, by describe, what I mean is predict. Let me explain this: language is used to control the world one lives in. Language is not necessary to experience. It describes, labels, defines, and so forth, only so that ego can communicate with ego the illusion that needs to be controlled. Control presupposes the need to predict. Language, like science, arises out of the need to predict, and therefore, provide some level of comfort through an illusion of controllability. We wish to predict how people will take us, what the weather will do, what will happen as the result of certain actions, and so forth. All this is the language of future and past. In NOW, or ONENESS, language is about as necessary as the proverbial 'tits on a boar'. So some so-called deep thinker contemplates the nature of the universe and begins to question infinite constructs with finite bullshit and the result is either contradiction or circularity. It's kinda like tryin' to measure the circumference of a one-inch circle with an audio meter. The tool is inept for the task. That's just a given, Doc, and a necessary one by nature of definition.

"Let me give ya' one more example just for fun. One of your philosophers, Kurt Goedel, argues that first principles cannot be proven. His argument is necessary and appropriate. The stuff of the big bang is no different than the stuff of God, in terms of logic. If the big bang is not answerable in terms of sufficient cause, then why should God be answerable in the same context? In other words, if it's science to accept the big bang without being able to justify the hows and whys of the whole matter, isn't it just a duck to attempt to use a different criteria to evaluate or judge God. I mean, in fact, doesn't the big bang necessitate a sufficient cause according to logic? If so, then doesn't that in and of itself perhaps push us out into the metaphysics Aristotle addressed? The answer is **yes**!

"Now Doc, this first principle, God, is also the first principle: **man**! You. Me. Us. All of us in the At-one-ment.

Okay Doc, is all this clear to you? I didn't think so, but it will get clearer as you deal with it. I've got to be off now, there's a little matter upstairs that I need to attend to. You keep readin' and thinkin' and I'll talk at ya' again soon."

"Dink, one more thing please."

"What's that Doc?"

"How does one integrate all of this information into being in God as you suggest?"

"I like the motivation Doc. Your question is straight forward and I'll give you a straight forward answer. You simply do what the shoe-salesman says, '**do it!**' Here is the practical application, just start teaching what I've told you. You are what you teach. Every communication, every action, every thought energy is either an investment in illusion, hell, delusion, or truth. Truth, remember, is eternal. Invest your thoughts, actions and so forth in truth. Act as though God exists in all. Walk in gratitude, forgive all, behold your own innocence; but above all else, teach that God is in all, that this world is an illusion, that the ego is false, that you are perfect because you were created perfectly, that all life matters, and further Doc, that nothing is outside of you!

"Now that last one deserves a tiny bit of qualification. Well actually, it deserves much more than that, but for now I'll just introduce the whole idea to ya'. Since we create our world, the fear or anger or guilt we sense is coming from us. When you think it is in someone else, it's really in you. You project this belief onto the world. The correct form of forgiveness requires acknowledging that there is nothing to forgive. Actually, and we'll talk about this more later, when you forgive, it is appropriate to repeat to yourself, 'I forgive old such-and-such for what they didn't do.' 'Cause remember Doc, it's your projection. Oh, but this will take a long time to explain, so you just sort of hold it in suspense until I speak with you again. Now, I've gotta get."

As usual, with no more amenity than that, the Dink was gone. I mused for a few moments over his last comment. "Suspense," he had said. "No shit," I thought, "in suspense." Then it occurred to me that the Dink had me using some of his vocabulary. Not only was I in suspense, trying to patiently hold an idea that I admit I did not wish to even entertain, but doing so in disbelief while cussing at the notion of so doing. Everything seemed circular at this point. I decided to quit—just quit thinking about the whole matter and do something that I could lose myself in. I decided to boot a "Lost in Space" video game on my computer and for the next hour or so I lost contact with the outside world in favor of the surrealistic drama on the screen. Then it occurred to me, suddenly and seemingly from nowhere, how much of life was really like the video game under my fingertips?

CHAPTER ELEVEN

The world of projection
lives on the screen
in which life's every drama
is seemingly the scene
of who we are,
what we'll be,
and where we've been.

"Hey Doc, you in there Doc?"

"In where Dink?"

"Still in your head, guy?"

"That's an interesting question, Mr. Dink!"

"You know, it's really all about this inevitable journey—but the journey has no distance. Catch my drift?"

"I don't think so."

"Well, let's do a little review work then. Ya' see, this here stuff you call the world, the 'real' world, is really just so much make believe. I know that sounds tough, but the idea is true. So listen, the world is exactly as man has created and continues to create it. It is the illusion of belief and ideas, no different than a holographic projection. Indeed, in many ways, the model of a holographic projection is more than your usual model. The principles involved, from the mathematics to the infolded information field of your nobel physicist David Bohm, are exact models for much of your current science. Consequently, and to continue, your perception is intimately involved with the collective expectation, which collectively organizes and creates both more of the expectation and the stuff you call 'reality'. Got it?"

"In principle, I can think that way at times. However Dink, it somehow lacks the virtue of truth when I smash my head against the cupboard door. The pain of the moment tends to deny this notion of a world generated in and by the collective minds of mankind."

"That's a good point Doc. But the point assumes that you participate in the general belief. For what would you think if instead of bumping your head, it just sort of passed through the cupboard door?"

"If that happened Dink, then I would find the entire holographic model just a little more acceptable."

"Doc, if your head were to pass through the door, what would have to happen first?"

"I give. Tell me, what would have to happen first?"

"Your belief would have to change. It's that simple, SIR! Just like those gurus in India, China and Tibet, just like those prophets in Palestine, in order to perform the so-called miracle, you must **know** the miracle is possible! You must **believe** that you have the power to alter your body's vibrational rate and literally speed the molecules up in such a way as to pass through dense matter. You must realize that the whole matter is the substance of ideas and that you are both the ideas and the "ideator," or idea creator."

"So I'm not only an allegation, I'm an allegator?"

"Exactly! In other words, you are watching the projection of the world as a movie, but you do not realize that you wrote the script, created the actors and actresses, designed the film, the camera, the screen and even the body you would run the projector and watch the movie with. The real you, is tucked away under or behind all this facade of difference. The idea of separation has been given so much power that you don't even have the ability to question its reality. How then can you begin to think of a state of consciousness in which separation simply does not, did not, and never will exist?"

"Assume that I wished to think of myself in some manner similar to what you suggest, and I'm not certain that I do because how does one think of themselves without a themselves, an ego, to think of? But assume that I did, how would I go about this process?"

"Doc, listen up. First, assume there was no ego. If there was no ego, would there be the pain and grief in the world?"

"I don't know. There's still that kitchen cupboard door. But what if we all had altruistic egos akin to say Mother Theresa or Simone Weil?"

"Okay, be difficult. Let's *assume* that you have an altruistic ego?"

"You don't have to make it sound like such a stretch."

"See! Even the most altruistic ego will still make judgments."

"What's that got to do with eliminating pain and grief?"

"Well, the ego gets to decide what's altruistic, for example. Isn't that presupposed in your notion of an altruistic ego?"

"Alright, I accept that."

"Well Doc, it's just a damn given, that if the ego judges what is altruistic and not, that there is something not altruistic. Whatever that something is, it is not right. Ah, Doc, now creeps in this stuff, right and wrong. Judgement. Well, you gotta be righter than someone that's wrong, so now you got to act right in order to not be wrong. Ah, shit Doc, but now you're different and opposed and yet the same and you need the support of those who are on the side of right to oppose them others who're wrong. One simple idea, an altruistic ego, and whammo, back in the world of difference, separation, defenses, allies, enemies and so on. Hell Doc, don't you think this whole process is predictable once man is given consciousness?"

"I understand the circularity, but Dink, it's tough to let go of ego. No, not tough . . . impossible, isn't it?"

"Oooh. We'll get to that in a minute Doc, what I want you to be aware of first, is this here notion that God gave man consciousness fully aware that man would separate and that's part of the whole plan, if you will. I mean, plan is not a good word here, but it will have to do since there isn't a word for what the entire matter is about. Still, it was inevitable that man would reflect on himself at some level and begin the journey into separation which ultimately and inevitably will collapse back into singularity: **GODNESS**. This my stubborn friend, is the journey without distance. You're in the journey now. The way out of the confusion is the way back in. The journey ends with the realized **GODHEAD**.

Now Doc, you can take this to the bank. Until and unless you accept the possibilities of what I am telling you, you will not, can not, escape the circularity of the old thought patterns. That damn ego is what Jesus called Satan when he said, 'Get thee behind me Satan'. Remember the circumstances . . . Satan, ego, promised the world of sensory gratification, if only Jesus would acknowledge him, Satan, ego, as the Master. The ego is desirous of protecting the illusion of Maya since the ego will cease to exist if you and the Father become one. Can you understand that Doc?"

"I understand," and I could feel the words of Dink and they felt right, "but, you must admit Dink, the whole undoing process you describe is easier to think about than do."

"Of course Doc, that there's a given too. The Christian Atonement was powerfully hard and painful. But with some folks, like you, the world is first cerebral. You got to know **why** somethin' works, you're not happy with just havin' the **how**. I mean Doc, you've spent so much time in your head that if you can't think about it, it ain't fun. Hell, you don't even get aroused until you've thought about three or four erotic scenarios first."

"Excuse me?"

"Ya' know, some people can just do it. Tell 'em to turn on the light with the switch, shit they don't care what makes the switch turn the light on, let alone think of what in the world electricity is. But that ain't you Doc. So I got the job of gettin' enough juice in your head for you to make the light come on. And Doc, you got to hurry up.

"What was that about arousal?"

"Now you been readin' that there *Course In Miracles*, but you ain't been doin' the exercises. If you learn all there is to learn about electricity, but you don't know where the light switch is, you're still goin' to be in the dark. So stop just reading and thinking! Do something! Follow them exercises. Okay Doc?"

"Alright Dink, I'll do that, but there was a subject earlier that I'd like to ask you a couple of questions about."

"I'd love to Doc, but I got to get to this here meetin'. You wouldn't believe what some of these here so-called friends of mine are tryin' to talk me into. I got to work some things out over here first. We'll talk again soon. Well at least soon in the great grand scheme of things. Okay?"

I didn't bother to answer Dink for by now I had become conditioned to his sudden departures. I always felt silly talking to myself when I thought he was still around.

"Doc, I said okay?"

"I thought you were gone Dink. You always just leave."

"Not always. So I said, okay?"

"Sure."

"Thanks Doc, I gotta be a little more patient with ya', but I also need to get some other-things straight. So it helps me if it's okay. Now I'm gone."

I didn't know what Dink meant by his last comments but I forgot them as I began to examine the exercises in the *Course In Miracles*. The very first lesson instructed me to apply the following idea twice during the day, "**Nothing I see in this room [on this street, from this window, in this place] means anything.**"

Chapter Twelve

Fear is fueled by falseness
Finding fault with truth.

"Well Doc, what do ya' think of pretendin' that nothin' is real, nothin' matters, everything is only an idea and so forth?"

Dink's voice entered my head in the midst of an exercise from the *Course In Miracles*. It was a pleasant Saturday afternoon. I looked up from my book at the clock. It was 3.48 p.m. I had been feeling, or trying to feel the meaning of repeating, 'These thoughts do not mean anything. They are like the things I see in this room [on this street, from this window, in this place].'

"Dink," I answered with a grin on my face, "You don't mean anything. You are like my thoughts which mean nothing and my thoughts are like the things in this room, on this street, from this window which do not mean anything."

"Well Doc, as usual, you're a little right on and little off. These things, as you put it, do not mean anymore than you make them mean. So, do they mean anything?"

"I think the idea is not to reduce the meaning, but rather to release the attachment one has to ideas and things, is it not Dink?"

"Good one, Doc. You got that right. And, as you might say, the operational word here is 'attachment'. You see, the Course is designed to lead you to the possible realization that this here world of yours is only an illusion. One big projection like we've talked. In fact Doc, one thing you ain't got to yet, but I'll sort of jump start ya' into, is the idea that only LOVE is eternal. Now here Doc, we are talkin' about the kind of LOVE God is and we is, not that conditional stuff, or co-dependent crap you're always trying to talk to your patients about. So look at it this way Doc, if you can give it away without attachment, it's real. Ya' know, you give love, advice, friendship and so forth away and it feels good and it comes back. But now Doc, try givin' money away and not just a dime or a dollar—say write out a check for one day's pay and give **that** away. If it feels like you've given up something, then Doc, you know you ain't got it yet, you're still attached and that makes you unreal."

"Wait Dink. Before you start into all that 'it means nothing' relativism, I have a question or two about some of the material and ideas you have suggested in the past. Mainly, if time is a so-called illusion, why are you always in such a hurry to be somewhere else?"

"Oh Doc, nothing escapes that steel-trap mind of yours, does it?"

"Let's not divert from the subject. You have me doing all sorts of things that somehow feel both natural and silly. Like reading this Course, and talking to thin air. These things would be just a little beyond the pale for most people, and I admit, for myself from time to time. So give me some clear answers. Why are you always in such a hurry if there is no such thing as time?"

"Hoo-boy—persistent this **time** aren't ya? Okay. Imagine a balloon Doc, it has an inner and an outer event possibility. That is, from the inside of the balloon there is spatial arrangement, length, width, and so forth. Three-dimensional reality is possible. Now imagine that this balloon is very large, say the size of the galaxy, or add as many more galaxies as you need in order for this balloon to be large enough for it to hold everything you have ever imagined, every thought you've had, read about or heard rumors of. Got it?"

"It's a big balloon."

"Alright, from inside the balloon there is a light source, say a sun, or let's pluralize it, suns, and as light passes some linear point within the balloon an observer makes an observation. Now this is important Doc, time does not exist except for the act of observation and the stuff you call light. Think about this. When you dream, in only a few moments, many days can pass. That is, the mind can compress linear events into moments that are far shorter than the ability to relate the events, let alone experience them outside of the dream. Yet you have experienced them within the dream. And some of these dreams can be so real that they seem to take control of thoughts, emotions and even actions. You know what I mean?"

"I follow you Dink."

"Okay, this dream sequence appears to have time that is different from the time an observer in a sleep laboratory would record. Get it?"

"Yes."

"Okay, now there are two questions inherent to this simple observation. First, which time is accurate, the time of the dreamer or that of the observer in our sleep lab? Second, how do these times differ?"

There was a long pause while I considered Dink's questions before he continued speaking, "So you see Doc, dreamer's experience time according to what they later report as sequential events. These sequences are what you interpret to be time. In this sense, time is in the mind. Understand that Doc?"

"I think so."

"Okay, now the other time, that of the observer, this time is recorded according to an independent criteria, the watch. The watch measures time according to the speed of light. Now as Einstein showed the world, time in this sense is relative. What's more, no two people ever participate in the exact same event. And what's more, the faster an object or individual travels in relationship to the speed of light, the slower the clock of the universe runs for that object or individual. Now I know you're familiar with all this, so let's go a step further. There are these anomalies in space your scientists call black holes. Now a black hole is simply matter collapsing upon itself. Well, matter, light and everything else. So you have this scientific view of a universe with your solar systems, galaxies, and so forth expanding, while at the same time within this expanding universe there exist these contracting universes or black holes.

"Awright, now you got yer 'event horizons', or threshold areas where the two, expanding and contracting worlds, interface. In these event horizons time neither expands or contracts, for light neither expands or collapses. In other words, time stands still. The light cannot escape, expand, nor does it collapse into the anti-matter stuff in a black hole.

"Now, imagine Doc, that somehow you and your space capsule

were thrown into one of these event horizons. Time literally, according to science, stands still. Yet you are doing this and that. Does time pass, or are you confusing the nature of 'activity' with time? In other words Doc, is your sequence of events time or is the speed of light time?"

"Maybe both are time Dink."

"Now Doc, you're the one that fancies himself somewhat of a scientist, so don't cop out on me. You know that time, according to your scientific mind, is relative to the speed of light. And if I told you it took thirty days for me to have one dream you'd probably inform me that it only seemed like thirty days, especially if you timed my rapid eye movement during dream sleep and found that according to your watch the entire event took only three minutes of *real* time. Right Doc?"

"Probably," I smiled as I answered, for Dink's scenario reminded me of a client who had insisted that she moved through time and dimensions much like those in a 'Freddy' horror film. At the time, I had tried to disabuse her of the notion, but now, I think I would have settled for just getting her to take the knife blades off of her fingers.

"Okay Doc, now movin' right along. So time is **not** activity. Let's go another step or two before I answer your question. We're still on the inside of this balloon, remember. But from the inside we have differentiated between activity and time. Now, what you got to also recognize is that your notion of time is event oriented. Folks out there don't think of time in terms of Einsteinian space, light speed, relativity and so forth. You know that old adage, 'the watched pot never boils'."

"I have heard it Dink. And make it a point to have no visible clocks in my office . . . at least none that my clients can see."

"Exactly! What this expresses is the common conventional folk-wisdom that time is somehow subjective. Einstein's model is objective, out there, and the 'watched pot' metaphor is subjective, in here, or within the individual. Got it?"

"I do know the difference between objective and subjective Dink!"

"Sure you do Doc, in an intellectual way. What I'm tryin' to show ya' is through the eyes of common sense. Just plain old cowboy common sense. So here Doc, in the subjective sense, time is also relative. But in this form of relative we are talkin' about what goes on in the mind. Waitin' for anything can seem to take forever, especially if one is anxious or in a hurry. Lot's of things go into this phenomena, but we'll deal with just a couple. When the mind is asked to be still, it talks more and more. You know those meditators Doc, they must first learn to still the mind. This is tough. Try it. Just take a moment and think nothing. Tell your mind to be still and see what happens. I'll pause and give you a moment to do this Doc. Now go on and try."

I closed my eyes and said "still" to myself. Immediately my thoughts began to race. "Still," I spoke again to myself and my inner mind spoke back yapping like a puppy that wants attention. "Still," and yet my undisciplined thoughts continued.

"Okay Doc, ya' see how difficult something as simple as this can be. Now, while you was doin' your thing, these thoughts of yours were coming in linear, or sequential, progression. This progression of thought could be said to be an activity. The sequential nature of this activity produces a before and after. In other words, you tend to view all this activity of thinking-doing-being-as having past, present and future. However Doc, there really isn't a present. Think about this. The minute you recognize a thought, you are reflecting on what just happened previously. It's over. The thought has come and gone. In micro-seconds, the event is over. Indeed, some of your scientist have demonstrated that every thought you ever have of a conscious nature is given to you by your unconscious. So, you think something like, 'It's a nice day'. But the moment you become aware of the thought, it is over, it has passed. So Doc, yer thinking is in the past. Or, in the alternative, you think of the future. Now your thought activity, or your recognition of the thought has itself already passed, but perhaps the thought is of something in the future. It's kinda like some of those patients of yours that spend their time worrying about what comes next, what might happen and so forth. As such, your thoughts are either in the future or in the past. Thinking in now does not exist. Let me repeat that Doc, thinking in now does not exist!

"When you are in **now**, there is no thought. Not as you know it anyhow. In the eternal **now**, there is nothing to think about. No thought. And yet, all thought. But **no** thinking.

"So let's go back to our balloon. From within the balloon skin we identified time and activity. One of the reasons we could do this is due to the boundary, or stuff we called the skin of the balloon. In other words, there exists in this model a limitation, or confined parameter from which all is derived in terms of measurement. But what about from the outside of the balloon? Let's just assume that the outside knows no limitation. Has no boundaries. Is not the stuff of the inside. Let's assume that there is no so-called speed of light. Suddenly, time is a nonsense notion. Only an illusion. Now let's assume that the thought of **ONE** consciousness is only in **now**. There is suddenly no activity of thought, at least in the sense you conceive it. No activity means no before and after. No before and after translates into no activity as you know it. Alas, time has no more meaning to you than when you're fully asleep.

"Now Doc, you ain't got there yet, but the Course teaches ya' that there's no time. It teaches that all you think you know is a projection of ego, self identification as separate from all else. The mind of ego then projects into the future or draws upon the past. This entire process provides the substance of the one big projection, or illusion, or Maya, as the Hindus say; the dream within a dream. Remember the model of virtual reality, where two guys enter the game and become so involved that they forget they are really outside the game. You participate in this stuff you call the world of shoes and ships and ceiling wax. 'Reality', you say. 'Virtual reality', I might emend.

"Okay Doc, now to your question. In a sense one can be in and out of the virtual reality at the same time. In a sense, indeed, most of us are. Now, if I'm in the same game with you, but I choose to be in still another game at the same time, this is possible. However Doc, if I choose to be outside of the game or games, I will withdraw my presence. Because there is no time, but since you are viewing the game as real with sequential events that constitute time, for you my withdrawal means that you must wait for some series of events to pass before you can play with me again. You see this as **waiting**. You sense this as **time**.

"Now Doc, back to what you called 'all that means nothing relativism'. If the entire thing, what you call reality, is indeed a projection, a game, a virtual reality, then none of it means anything. Get it?"

"Little by little, I think."

"Okay, now Doc, try to live in the moment and keep up them there exercises from the Course. You'll see. I mean, remember that first exercise when you said everything meant nothing and it seemed like the ceilin' in your bedroom disappeared. Then ya' said, as ya' looked at the sky, this too means nothing and the sky disappeared. Then ya' said, this too means nothing and the sky became deep space. Don't ya' get it Doc? Your mind is so conditioned to think in linear terms that you went from ceiling to sky to space and so on. Now what if there just is one big void beyond what ya' think exists as real? What would this be? You think on that Doc.

"But before I leave ya', I want to tell you one of my favorite stories that may help ya' sort of live in the moment. Now Doc, maybe I should also tell ya' that these stories are not all original with me. I don't remember where this one came from, but ya'll like it. And ya' know, these damn stories er, parables some calls 'em, are quite the teachers.

"Okay, seems there was this here Zen monk. Everyday he made it a practice to walk in the jungle and meditate on nature during lunch time. Well, one day he wanders too far and comes upon a hungry tiger. Now ya' know, these here Zen monks spend lifetimes working on being in the moment, in the now. So our Monk gets into now in a real hurry and he runs with the hungry tiger in pursuit.

"Pretty quick this here Monk comes to a sheer cliff. It's too far down to jump and survive, but the hungry tiger is almost on him. So, in the moment, without future thinking, he jumps.

"Now on the way down he grabs the only growth on the side of the cliff, a small tree. Hangin' onto one of it's limbs he hears the hungry tiger's growl from above joined by a hungry tiger's growl from below. Hungry tiger above. Hungry tiger below.

"Then our ol' Zen master hears the small tree roots as they tear and break away from the side of the cliff. Well, he looks to his left. Nothin'. He looks to his right, and there's a beautiful and succulent strawberry plant with a ripe glowing strawberry. So he picks it and eats it. And ya' know, it was the best strawberry of his life.

"Now here's some of the moral Doc. Some folks in that situation would look at the strawberry and think they was crazy to even consider pickin' it. Hell man, whoops, excuse me **SIR**! Heavens! A tiger above and a tiger below want ya' for lunch. I ain't pickin' no strawberries. So they miss out on the best one of their lives.

"Now ya' know what else Doc? Some folks would look at that there strawberry and think to themselves, 'shit, looks good but I got this here allergy to strawberries'. As if it really mattered at a time like this.

"So Doc, pick the strawberries. Stay in the moment. Do all that ya' can to enjoy **now**. Don't worry. Don't complicate everything with all this here future/past thinkin'. Don't confuse the truth by measuring it with the tools of the false. Just kick back and be. Let it happen. Go with the flow. It'll help ya' get there. Look at it this way, if it helps guy, tomorrow you can go back to bein' one of them there thinkers. Tomorrow you can go back to havin' a day of worry. Tomorrow, you can go back to all this ordinary shit you ain't never found satisfyin', but ya' don't seem to want to give up either. For today, do the **now** stuff.

"Okay Doc, one more thing. Item: the baby's gonna change your life. Get ready. This little one will need ya' And you owe him."

"Does that mean it's a boy?"

"Just a figure of speech Doc. The sex stuff ain't yet all worked out. I'll keep ya' advised though. Now I'm really, really late so I'm out of here. ."

"Yes, see ya' Dink."

What did I mean by that? I never saw the Dink, only heard him. I wondered, could he show himself? I looked back to my book, "These thoughts do not mean anything." I checked the clock. 3:49 p.m.

CHAPTER THIRTEEN

Being is about caring,
For when you're able to care more
About another than yourself,
Then and only then—
Will you find and know yourself.

"Hey Doc, you're doin' right good. I've been sorta monitorin' your progress and I'm proud of ya'."

"Thank you, but I am not as confident. Some of this feels very comfortable, and I will admit that it has aided me. I am much more at peace with myself now and most of my clients have benefitted as well."

"So what's the problem?"

"Dink, I am unable to conceptualize or conceive of this nothing that is everything. I am not sure that I truly wish to let go of my illusions including my ego. I mean, what then? Just a great big void?"

"No Doc, not at all. But to get to the heart of it we'll have to take a round about course. So let's begin with something easy.

"Remember when you came upon that fellow who'd just been hit by a car? The one who was ridin' his scooter. The old guy. Remember?"

"Yes, I do."

"Okay, remember little hesitation before you helped. You had all them there thoughts about maybe bein' sued. Then you just got in and felt for broken bones, elevated his legs and all that. Remember?"

"Yes."

"Okay Doc, while you were helping this man, did you think anymore about yourself?"

"No, there wasn't time for that."

"Course not. That's part of my point. While you were helpin', you were unable to think selfish thoughts. In fact, when you're totally into that moment, going to the aid of another, in the midst of a life and death emergency, you don't think of yourself at all. Now do you Doc?"

"No, I didn't. Oh, maybe some, but no, that is either just before or right after you do what must be done."

"Good Doc, we'll get there, and who knows, maybe even today. So, in that moment of doing, do you feel pain if you've been hurtin'. You know, emotional or physical pain?"

I knew that I did not, because I had once been involved in a situation where while I was helping another, my own pain disappeared. "No Dink, you don't."

"Right again, Doc. Indeed, when you truly seek to aid another who is suffering, you tend to lose yourself. Now what's more Doc, when you are aiding someone in need, in pain, in peril, someone that you love, then the loss of self is even more intense. At the moment of urgency, there is only the awareness of the other's needs. Would you agree with this?"

"Yes, I know from my own experience that you're right. In fact, not only is this true, but Dink, I don't think you even consider your own risk or need at times like those."

"True, true, Doc. Only in 20-20 hindsight does a person begin to think of self in these scenarios. Now, let's go one step further by going a step or two back. Remember the ol' guy, hit by the car, the one we talked about earlier?"

"Yes."

"Do you remember how you felt after the crisis?"

"Yes. In fact, I remember it all quite clearly."

"Why is that Doc?"

"I guess because I've rarely felt so good and inexpressibly positive about anything like that before—or since. I had a certain type of euphoria. A cleansing and an enrichment of myself, my soul, or whatever. I felt extremely positive about refusing to withdraw aid from fear of lawsuits, or whatever. The man lived and was not permanently crippled. I believe I had a role in that. I even remember giving thanks to Whomever Above, God, I guess, for the opportunity to help this man."

"Oh Doc, you do please me at times. That last comment gives

me ghost goose bumps, ya' know, goose bump memories. Fer ya' see Doc, you already know through experience what it is to lose yourself in the so-called 'void'. What it is, the at-one-ment, atonement, is a loss of self in the LOVE of another. Ironically Doc, this loss of self is the only way you gain yourself. Indeed, you cannot know yourself until you've lost yourself in the precise manner that we have been speaking. That unconditional LOVE manner. You know, you didn't know this ol' guy in the accident, but you cared for him as though you did. When you see good, or as some say, God in all, then you act as though the good or God mattered. When you do this, you lose and gain yourself in the process. Got it Doc?"

"I think so, Dink. I think so."

"Okay Doc, now one more thing. You gotta remember to do these lessons in that Course everyday. Do two a day from here on in. You're runnin' out of time. Ya' got to get this stuff in order before that little one in Momma's hopper comes in. Right from the git-go, ya' got to help this little one with what you learned. Got it?"

"Is it all that important Dink?"

"Yes Doc, it is! This here little one is special. He's very special to you and me. So no more goofing' off on yer homework. Git them studies done."

"I'll start on two a day tomorrow. Does that make you happy?"

"Happy as a honey bee in tall clover."

"Okay Dink, you have my word."

"On that then Doc, I'll leave ya'. Just remember what ol' Martin Luther King said, 'Ya'll never be what ya' ought to be until all us others is what we ought to be.' Well, he said it more eloquently than that, but you get the jist."

"That I do Dink. His precise words were, 'I can never be what I ought to be until you are what you ought to be . . . "

"Yeah, I knew that Doc. But I just sort of figure I'll eloqute the way I does for a bit longer while I still can."

"What do you mean?"

There was no answer. The Dink had left. Like the trickster personality archetype of Carl Jung's, once again he came with annoying questions and manners of speech, only to leave me with novel methods of perception and insights not formerly entertained.

CHAPTER FOURTEEN

Fear is self-deceit
Whose only harvest reaps
A toil with seeds
Like anger, lust and greed;
Such stuff on what we feed.

"Well Doc, how ya' been?"

"Hello Dink. I wondered how much longer before you returned. I'm doing very well. The Course is making a lot of sense now. Not only that, it feels good."

"I'm proud of ya' Doc. You do good. Anything I can help ya' with?"

"Perhaps. I have been looking at the Bible some as I work with the Course. There are a couple of things I'm not quite clear on."

"Okay, give me a shot."

"This entire idea of heaven and hell, God and Satan, from the Biblical material seems to be in direct contradiction with the Course."

"Not really Doc. Your choice of the word 'seems' is a good one.

For ya' see, the typical interpretation of heaven, hell and so forth is incorrect. In fact, it's so flawed that it's sometimes difficult to believe that anyone really holds these crazy notions.

Let me see if I can make this all somewhat more clear. Let's start with the idea of hell. Ya' know, originally the language used to describe hell simply meant grave like the Hebrew word *Sheol* or the Greek word *Hades*. But then along came this wonderful metaphor, and the ol' Rabbi's did like powerful metaphors, teaching stories and parables. In fact, they really used these methods to exaggerate their points. This exaggeration your theological scholars call 'rabbinic hyperbole'. Now what happened Doc, there was this here ditch called the Valley of Hinnom. It was just a little southwest of Jerusalem. Now for years the valley had been a cite of desecration. In fact, it was once used to burn children in sacrifice to Molech, the Ammonite God. Well, the folks of Jerusalem denounced this practice and eventually gave the valley the name ge-hinnom. Later this word was translated into the Greek word 'gehenna' meaning hell. Now if you think of this valley, a place for years where fires burnt children in sacrifice and later a garbage refuge with fires burning dead bodies and what not, ya' can see real easily why Jesus might refer to hell as ge-hinnon. I mean the imagery of this valley is terrifyin', ya' see?"

"So, what you're saying Dink, is something like, Jesus never taught there was a hell per se'?"

"Exactly Doc. Jesus never taught anything about a jealous and vengeful God or a real live bowel called hell. In fact, as we've discussed, he taught that heaven was within, and ya' might add, the realm of hell could likewise be within. When he cast out the devils, where were they?—Within the person, eh. Ya' see, man's ignorance of who he is causes him to suffer in a world of conflict. This conflict is created by the idea that man is separate from his fellow man and God. And what did the poor feller filled with hell say his name was? "Legion, for I am many." The ego generates this here separation stuff, and then perpetuates it all by projecting fear. Now ol' C.S. Lewis said something like, hell is the absence of heaven. And he's right, guy. Only I'd say, hell is the absence of peace. But now, let me take this a little further.

"Let's take ol' Satan. Ya' know, Peter tells Jesus in Matthew that he doesn't need to go through with this here crucifixion stuff, and Jesus tells Peter, 'Get thee behind me Satan'. Now you don't think Jesus thought Peter was literally Satan, do ya'?"

"No."

"Ya' don't think that ol' Satan had just possessed Peter do ya?"

"No."

"Now think about it. We also read in Matthew that Jesus was tempted in the desert by Satan and that ol' Scratch showed Jesus all the glories of the world he could have if he gave up this God idea. Remember?"

"Yes."

"Okay, now if you was to say to yourself, I'm givin' up all this here worldly stuff, I'm goin' be a better human bein', I'm not goin' become angry or fearful, I'm goin' love and trust everyone, what do you think your ol' ego would say?"

"Probably something like, you can't trust everyone and so forth."

"Now what if you convinced the ol' ego that you really didn't need him any longer, for you were a child of God in the one eternal Sonship of God, perfect and loved. Like the prodigal son story in the Bible, you simply correct your view of the stuff ya' think of as important and real, and find that God welcomes you with an open-armed feast and treats you as though ya' never left his home. Now, what do ya' think ol' ego is about to do?"

"Probably start telling me how crazy I am, what I'll be missing, why I'm deluded in my thinking, and so forth. Or maybe like the brother of the prodigal, ego would say, 'What about me—don't you care about me?'"

"Very insightful Doc. That's exactly what Jesus found. When the thoughts are focused on this world above all else, the animal man, the so-called i, when those thoughts are driven by fear, guilt and all that so-called real world stuff, then ego is needed to protect ya'. Ego needs you to need it, remember Doc?"

"I understand. So what you are saying Dink, is that Satan is the ego?"

"Exactly Doc. Satan is the deceiver. The voice that speaks to you of fear, for it comes only from fear. Fear that you are somehow faulty. Then the fear that you are faulty, stupid, ugly and so forth, generates this protection system which must perpetrate some of the fear in order to be needed. Alas, Doc, that co-dependence we talked about pops up its head. The ultimate in co-dependent relationships is with the ego. And Doc, as with any co-dependence, or neurotic behavior, this relationship is destructive. It nurtures a false sense of self that depends upon the ego or another to provide its worth, its protection and so forth. It's a controlling, manipulative, anger/fear based existence. Now Doc, if this ain't hell I don't know what you'd call it. It damn sure ain't heaven or peace.

"So ya' see Doc, hell is a realm within, just as heaven is, and the so-called tempter or deceiver some call satan is really the ego. This ego function keeps one acting in a lower-self, or un-actualized self, perpetuating an illusion of co-dependent need, separation, and thereby keeping one from actualizing the higher self. Kinda reminds me of this here poem that some anonymous writer wrote years ago:

"Within my earthly temple there's a crowd;
There's one of us that's humble, one that's proud;
There's one that's broken hearted for his sins
And one who, unrepentant, sits and grins;
There's one who loves his neighbor as himself
And one who cares for naught but fame and pelf.
From such corroding care I would be free
If once I could determine which is me."

"Well inside each of us is this lower un-actualized delusional self, this ego and our real self. Think that way Doc. Not the ego, id and super ego, but an un-actualized, an ego, and an actualized real self. The actualized real self is selfless. It is the Christ consciousness, or Christ self. What an irony, huh Doc?"

"Not really. But it is a good paradox. It's sort of like saying you must give up what you think is yourself in order to find yourself."

"That's it Doc. And the best way to do that is by loving others and maintaining an attitude of gratitude. Just go around sayin' thank you for everything that comes along and see how fast your life changes. Just that one switch in the head will get ya' out of many of those ol' ruts most folks have been in. Try with your clients too, Doc."

"That's a good idea Dink. I'll do that."

"So Doc, heaven, the peace that passeth understanding, comes from within and resides in the moment of realization that you and the Father are One, as are all in the One Sonship. Hell is the absence of peace. Satan is the ego and God is all that is real and eternal, which includes the One Sonship, you and me and all others, for God created us, and the Holy Spirit, which you didn't ask about, but is essential for us to successfully remember who we are, is the spirit of communication, the essence of the exchange between God and man. It's really so simple, ya' see Doc?"

"It makes a lot more sense than all this wrathful, vengeful God stuff. I've always had problems with that part of typical Christian orthodoxy. In fact, I have often wondered if one should worship such a God just because he is God, or if there wasn't a higher moral imperative that demanded defying such a tyrant."

"Well Doc, most people now a days have some similar problem with this nonsense. It's that old bullshit, love God 'cause if ya' don't he'll burn ya' in the fires of hell. Closer to the truth would be, love yourself as God or you will make yourself think you're miserable."

"So Dink, what next?"

"Practice this here miracle mindedness that the Course teaches. Keep up with those lessons for they'll help you experience more than the illusion. Stay with it for a while more and we'll talk again."

"I'll do it."

"Now Doc, I've got a question for ya. Does you and momma want a boy or a girl?"

"I don't know. We're like everybody else, we want a healthy baby."

"Ya' got that Doc. But if ya' had your druthers, would you druther it be a boy or a girl?"

"For me, probably a boy."

"Thanks Doc. That means more to me then ya' know."

"I don't understand."

"I know, but ya' will in time. I'm takin' this news back now, so I'm out of here—okay?"

"Sure. But come back soon, okay Dink?"

"Ya' kinda gittin' fond of me, aren't ya' Doc?"

"Yes, I'd say that's true Dink."

"Me too, Doc. But that's enough of that mushy stuff fur now. See ya Guy."

"Ya, see ya' Dink. Oh, wait a minute Dink."

But he was gone. I decided to prompt myself with a note. The next time I speak with Dink, I must ask him if I could ever see him.

CHAPTER FIFTEEN

Forgiving teaches
there is nothing to forgive.

I had awakened from a dream disturbed. The imagery was so vivid and real that I decided to work on interpreting the dream. I left my wife sleeping and sat down behind my desk to recollect as many of the dream's details as I could.

The dream had elements that were very comforting, although in some intangible way. Yet, there were elements that felt good but still disturbed some part of my psyche.

A personal dream full of laughter and joy with many unknown characters seemed merged somehow in other personal dreams which collectively created one dream. The boundaries of the dreams became so obtuse at times that the entire dream seemed as though it were only a faint illusion; a mirage in a desert where although my eyes told me water existed, I nevertheless knew that it did not. A dream within dreams within **a** dream, what was real?

I had read many times of Eastern thought regarding illusion; a world known as Maya, sometimes even referred to as a dream within a dream. Still, the words had never been more than abstract thoughts to consider before Dink came into my life.

Here I sat, feeling the illusion. I reached for my pen laying on top of the desk in order to begin to write some of my thoughts. As I did, my mind and eyes were un-focused, still somewhat in the dream of dreams. I moved my hand to feel my pen, it was not there. I looked. Suddenly my heart raced. I jerked my hand away from the desk and my body trembled. My hand and part of my arm had been inside the desk. I had reached through the desk as though it were only a projection of light registered in my mind as a solid. I reached back to my desk. It was solid. Had I imagined reaching through my desk?

"Dink," I uttered in a half whisper, "if you're around, I could use some help."

"Right here Doc," the voice answered.

"Thank God you heard me. I think I'm getting a little too enmeshed in all this stuff. I would have sworn that I just put my hand and part of my arm right through my desk. And I mean through, like right into it as if it were a fluid, or just a light reflection."

"You did Doc. That's exactly what you did. And it happened because for a moment, you were aware, you remembered, that the entire affair you usually think of as real, is only an illusion; a dream within dreams within **a** dream. For that moment, that your hand was in your desk you were in the world but not of it. Get it Doc? You were walking on water."

"Come on Dink, that can't be real!"

"What do you mean by real Doc?"

"Objectively real."

"Objective, subjective, pototo, potato! Let me tell you about those so-called realities. The collective reality is first a collective agreement. God created man/mind. Therefore the only thing with which you can create is mind. If you think about it for a moment, the most complicated achievements are first created in the mind. Now mind, or minds, agree to enroll in this illusion you call world by the very same process that each and all came to the separation. That question, what am I, produced this world of separation. Remember, we talked about this?"

"I remember, but that is not what I mean."

"I know perfectly well what you mean Doc, just let me get there. Sometimes you can be so damned impatient. Just keep your pants on a minute and I'll get ya' to your answer.

"Once a collective belief is agreed on, and comes into being it sets out what you might compare to the rules of the game in our old analogy of this all bein' in the simulator we called virtual reality. So, this here collective belief becomes the objective reality. Objective in the sense that every so-called sane person agrees that it is more or less real. 'Cause ya' see, Doc, this objective reality is also subject to the subjective interpretation of it. Thus, objective stuff is subjectively agreed to be objective. Now subjective stuff is that part of the personal creation which interprets the *meaning* of objective this an that. So ya' see, objective simply means agreed to, and subjective simply means private interpretation and re-interpretation of the agreement. Neither are real, for inherently they are only the products of separation. When confusion ceases, so does the so-called necessity for this here world of things which, when given enough belief, appears real. In other words, for a moment, you did not perceive of the 'real' as real and when your perception shifted, truly shifted, so did the belief, and ergo, out went the stuff you used to think was real. You did indeed put your hand into and through a solid substance only because to you, at that moment, there was no such thing as a solid substance; let alone an agreement regarding what was real."

"Dink, do you know how many patients I have had that claimed to be beyond the real?"

"Twenty-seven, but Doc, don't confuse the matter. That's your ego sayin' look out, you need me to protect you from this far-out shit. And that's you sayin' something like, 'Right, I do need you ego,' and the whole matter of the ego-you co-dependent roles get deemed necessary. You know better Doc. When ya' have an experience, like the kind ya' just had, to deny it is to insist on staying in some so-called safe place. Ya' see, if ya' accept and integrate that there experience, somethin' fundamental is gonna shift. That means change. Big time change! Saying bye-bye to yer comfort zone. Leaving the womb. That's scary, ain't it Doc?"

"Dink, maybe it is fear that compels me to wish that the whole thing, dream and desk and perhaps even you, never happened. But I'll tell you something right now, I'm not too awfully comfortable with what's going on."

"So, who promised you a rose garden? You feel good about some things and nervous about others. Git used to it. There are two kinds of pain or discomfort in the world. One is degeneration and the other is regeneration. Doc you're regeneratin'. Growin'. Rememberin'. It's good fer ya'. What's more Doc, in yer heart of hearts, ya' know it. Ya' want it. Ya' been searching' fer it for sometime. So take a deep breath and realize, ya' just had one of them there mystical moments ya' said ya' always wanted, 'cause then you'd know it's okay to believe in

God and the eternal. Ya' just got yer wish Doc. Ain't it grand."

I had to laugh. The damn Dink was right. How many times I had desired, wished, fantasized about having a mystical experience. Then one comes along, and what do I do? Run frightened in denial from the entire matter. "Yeah, simply grand Dink—I think—maybe."

"Oh Doc, what is a fella to do with ya'? You just were in one of those special moments of being in the world and not of the world. It ought to mean something. Just take that meaning and ruminate a little. That's all I ask. Keep workin' with the Course, and see what happens. But speakin' of the Course, Doc, don't get so all-fired uppity about this forgiveness stuff. I know ya' been doin' a lot of thinkin' about how much you've grown and how far you've come, but don't git to thinkin' you're better'n anyone else. As soon as ya' do that, ya' show your ignorance. It's kinda like some of them spiritual and religious healers, Doc. They sometimes tend to think of the sick as different from themselves. They believe they have some special gift, and what happens is they lose sight of the true miracle. 'Cause ya' see, Doc, the miracle exists because we are all one in the Sonship. God has given all of us the same gifts.

"Remember that your gifts are not any different than the gifts of others. Likewise, when you forgive someone, there really is nothing to forgive. You are only correcting your perception of things, and I probably should say, mis-perception. When you see God in all, then you recognize that different people are just in different places, or relative states of awareness. In the One Sonship, there exists only perfection, for that is all that God created. In that Sonship, you and everyone else is perfect already. In this Sonship state of awareness, or Christ awareness, there is no confusion. As such, there aren't questions like, 'what's real.' For in this state, you just are. clarity, subjective, objective, you versus me, and so forth, all these dichotomies or differences cease to be relevant. They are observations by the confused about confusion only. So Doc, since all this real world stuff, which is a product of man's creation through projection, his collective belief, and so forth, is not ultimately real, has no more meaning than you give it, then what is real is perfect. Thus, when you forgive, your act is really an act of forgiving what didn't really happen and therefore, forgiveness is not necessary. No, indeed. Forgiveness is only a step in the realization process. It releases one from binding ties that serve only to reinforce the ego illusion: **separation**!

"Now ya' got all that Doc?"

"Yes. And I do believe that I feel the correctness, even if sometimes I fail to understand why."

"Don't worry Doc. If you truly feel it, the understanding will come. Only this time, it will be true understanding—not the illusory stuff sometimes called learned response, a system of contrived mechanical responses. And a lot of so-called learning is no more than that. Memorize the rules, reason from them, and I guarantee ya' Doc, your conclusion is foreordained. Git out of those rules and believe me, reason's beauty is beheld in their release. And by that Doc, I mean it is no longer necessary, for there is nothin' to reason, no confusion, no mystery, and what's left is simply **wow**!"

"Okay Dink. Thank you. You help me to believe in the process, at least enough to continue. For that I am indebted."

"Oh, just remember that Doc, fer I've got a surprise comin' your way."

"What surprise?"

"Maybe next time Doc."

"One other thing Dink, since I sense you're about to leave. Can I ever see you?"

"You mean with your eyes Doc?"

"Exactly."

"Real soon now. But that's part of your surprise. So jist hold yer britches. More to come later."

"Thanks Dink."

"Fer sure, Doc."

I went back to bed. My dream continued as though there had been no interruption. However, this time nothing disturbed me. I was at peace with some level of knowing what had taken place in me. I could not put it all in words, but somehow, perhaps in a noetic way, I fundamentally knew that I had made some realization that would forever alter the manner in which I interpreted my world.

Chapter Sixteen

Teach peace, and peace is yours.
Teach love, and what you'll have is love.
Pretend to be what you wish to be
And tomorrow, what you'll be, is what you
pretended only yesterday to be.

"Hey Doc, I need a moment or two of your time."

"Hello Dink, you've got it."

"I want to summarize some things with ya' Doc. Okay?"

"Sure, good. Go ahead." Dink had arrived at an opportune time for me. In fact, I was just missing the fellow when he spoke up. His voice had now become so familiar and warm that it was almost like having a treasured loved one speak to you.

"Doc, you're doin' well. I know you've had some difficult times and all, but again, I'm right proud of ya'."

"Thanks Dink. I do feel like I have somewhat of a handle on it all now, and I must tell you that I am very grateful for your leadership. I am also grateful for all the help in assisting me with some of my mental obstacles."

"I'd ask how grateful, but I'll hold that for later. So let's run this here refresher. First Doc, LOVE is all there is. That is the only lesson to learn. The separation is false. God is LOVE, you is LOVE, we all is only LOVE. Know that, and you know it all. You are one in the One Sonship of God. We are all one in the One Sonship.

"Second, teach what you want to be. What you teach is who you become. Pretend if you need to, but teach Love Doc, only Love.

"Third, the only sin is separation. The at-one-ment comes in remembering that you are in the body of God, in the One Sonship. In that at-one-ment, the illusion of separateness disappears as does the confusion. Clarity presides. The peace that passeth understanding is known.

"Fourth, what you resist you become. Resistance is ego. It is separation. It vests power in an illusory world. Be grateful for everything. Walk in the awareness that any other view is irrational. Irrational because it produces only conflict.

"Fifth, anger is only a call for love. All those feelings of inadequacy are only calls for love.

"Sixth, remove the fear and what remains is love. Remove the distinction, you verses the world, and ego has no place. Remove ego and the thought pattern which produces the illusion of separation is corrected.

"Seventh, the only judgement God makes is already made in the creation. As such, judgement only means correction. Correction in thinking ends suffering, for it ends the illusion. What remains is the eternal Oneness, in the One Sonship of God, which is perfect LOVE.

"Eighth, live life in joy. Take advantage of the opportunity to celebrate the liberation. Living in LOVE is joyous. Gratefulness celebrates the glory of you. You are a miracle.

"Ninth, miracles are natural. The un-natural is the world of illusion full of scarcity and separation. What you can give away and be enriched by is what has been given in LOVE. Any other gift is conditional at best, for if the act of giving tends to produce the feeling of loss, then the act is still in separation. A true gift is one that enriches. Miracle mindedness perceives this correctly. Any gift to another is a gift to self.

"Tenth, it can't be done alone. It takes two or more for the separation idea to be erased. When you behold the One Sonship in which you have your being, as the same One Sonship in which all others have theirs, when you do this with just one other person, miracles occur. In that holy moment, there is no separation. You just **is,** my friend, and **Isness** just **is**.

"Ya' see Doc, all this stuff helps you evaluate your values, which leads to a new level of perception; let's say corrected perception. All those **Course** exercises in the beginnin', like 'these thoughts mean nothing', are about teaching you through yourself that everything in the world you call reality is constructed according to your values. Things and situations mean nothing more than what you interpret them to mean. You place the meaning and value on all this stuff that seems to control the thoughts and behavior of so many folks. And indeed, Doc, all these things are meaningless, unless you say otherwise. The only meaningful anything is in the One Sonship.

So, the Course sort of helps ya' see things differently. It's kinda like an ol' story I remember hearin'. Jist imagine that you was walkin' down a street, let's say in a big city, oh Manhattan. Now, imagine that this here flower pot falls from a third story balcony above yer head. It smacks ya right on the noggin, pot breaks and falls to the sidewalk. Now you got some choices Doc. Ya' see, you can look at this here high rise condominium and know that the folks livin' there got lots of bucks. So, hey, ya' can throw yerself down on the sidewalk and fake big time injuries. Sue them suckers and get some big money fer yer pain. Or, let's see, Doc, ya' could take that ol' flower and broken pot upstairs and shove it up you know whose you know what. That'd teach the old fart not to put the flower pot so close to the edge of the balcony. 'Course ya' could git up there and find out it's a beautiful woman and change yer mind; or, it could be some mammoth dude in a bad mood that's right glad to have ya' stop by all pissed off. He can git his problems out of his system by poundin' on yer face a little. So, this choice may not be as good as ya might think.

"Well, what else could ya' do? Let's see. Ya' could sort of pretend it didn't happen. Ya' know, get one of them there metaphysical perspectives: everything happens fer some reason. Heck, who knows, maybe the blow to yer head delivered enlightenment. Huh? It happened to Edgar Cayce and Isaac Newton.

"But, my point is this: What will ya' do? What other choices are there? Try this Doc, you could take that flower to the florist, re-pot it, and then take it back to the owner as a gift of love. Hey the flower would like that. And the florist and the person who dropped it.

"Now Doc, which of these choices do ya' think would minimize the conflict in yer life and maximize the joy?"

"Probably the last choice."

"That's right Doc, pure practical shit tells ya' that. But to be able to make this choice, ya' have to be able to think differently than most folks. The Course helps ya' see what's truly important, and in that way, ya' empower yourself with the ability to make correct choices. 'Cause ya' see Doc, incorrect choice is only confusion. That's why the words, 'choose once again'. It's all about that, and one day, there ain't no choice to make, fer there ain't no confusion.

"Now Doc, I could go on, but that's the jist of it. Okay?"

"Yes Duncan."

"Hey Doc, no Duncan stuff!"

I smiled, "Alright Dink. I do understand. I'll tell you something else Dink, applying the philosophy of Love produces amazing practical results."

"Ain't it wonderful Doc?"

"Yes it is. I have seen some miraculous changes in patients and my own life as a result of applying this shift in perspective."

"You ain't seen nothin' yet."

"What do you mean by that?"

"Remember that there surprise I been promisin' ya'?"

"I do indeed."

"Well Doc, ya' know little momma's about to pop."

"Yes. Are you going to tell me whether it's a boy or a girl?"

"That too Doc."

"What do you mean?"

"You remember when I was havin' to always skeedadle out of here in a hurry?"

"Sure."

"Well Doc, there was this here heavy duty conversation goin' on about whether or not you were goin' to get a boy or a girl. I finally persuaded them. Actually, you tellin' me that ya' wanted a boy tipped the scale in my favor."

"Thanks Dink, I guess."

"Well it wasn't just fer you Doc that I worked so hard at gettin' a boy. Ya' see, Doc, I didn't want to come back as a girl. No way man! Not the way the world is set up against women. Life is hard enough."

"Wait a minute. Are you telling me that you're coming into this world as my son?"

"Don't sound so all-fired alarmed Doc. Ya' said ya' wanted to see me with your own eyes, didn't ya'?"

"I didn't mean in that manner Dink."

"Be careful what you wish for. But don't worry, it'll be good

Doc."

I didn't know what to say. I think I must have been in some form of temporary shock. When it wore off, Dink was gone. The entire Dink affair seemed like a dream. Indeed, many dreams within a dream. Did it all really happen?

The *Course In Miracles* laid on my desk where I had placed it. I opened the book. As I read from page one, the material seemed all so familiar. Had I read this before? I pulled at my beard, puzzled. Dream? Somehow, I felt as though everything had happened, and yet, somehow, it could have all been my imagination. And in my heart, I knew there was no difference between the two alternatives.

CHAPTER SEVENTEEN

Dreams co-mingle
With daytime pursuits;
Boundaries only
Create different suits
That each will wear,
But in difference, becomes
The cross, they shall bear.

We named our son James Duncan. Both his first and middle name had special meaning to me. James for my grandfather, and Duncan for the Dink.

James grew rapidly. He was bright and full of energy. Everyday was a new challenge and a new miracle. Just beholding him grow moved me so deeply that at times it seemed to take my breath away.

My professional practice prospered. I now taught what I had learned from Dink. It no longer bothered me whether he was real or not. The teachings stood on their own results. The Course was a part and parcel of who I had become. Like so many before me, it so changed my life to such an extent that in looking back, I sometimes doubted that I had ever been in some of the states of mind that memory indicated had been mine. I knew I still had room for improvement, and I also knew I had no answer for "how high is up." I also knew, I was up a long ways from where I had been in the pre-Dink era.

There were times that I experienced those "holy moments" Dink had spoken of. Each time lasted longer and I knew the shift was still taking place in me. I was finally at peace with myself.

"Dad," James spoke, "could you hypnotize me? I'm really nervous about the test tomorrow."

"James, my wonderful son, it's only a general intelligence test. They give it to all children entering school."

"I know Dad. You told me all that, but I don't want to go to bed and worry about it again tonight."

"James, there's nothing to worry about. It doesn't matter what you score. Just do your best. Everything will be okay. I love you and nothing will change that."

"Please Dad. Just hypnotize me and relax me like you do with your clients."

"Okay James, come over here and lay down on the sofa."

I did a progressive relaxation for James and then counted him down to a special place inside himself where peace prospered, only peace and joy. I was about to begin to suggest positive feelings and expectations regarding tomorrow's test when an old and familiar voice spoke to me through the mouth of my son.

"Hi ya' Doc, how ya' been? Long time no talk. Ya' does remember me don't ya Doc? This here is Dink, not Duncan, Doc! How dare you name me Duncan!"

I had been waiting for this and knew just what to say. "I called you Duncan so that your Self, which, like the lotus that blossoms only in polluted waters or the sunset whose full spectrum is beautified by polluted skies, might grow more beautiful and radiant because of its humble and undignified name. Duncan!"

"Smart-ass!"

OTHER BEST SELLING BOOKS FROM R.K. BOOKS

The Jaxon Files by Tony Markham - an entertaining and thought-provoking spiritual thriller by a master of language.

Life Beyond Death by Henk Giebels - the Archangel Michael communicates through a business man and non-believer.

SelfPower by Eldon Taylor - a practical persons guide to mysticism and psychology. This book is full of exercises that will change your life.

Exclusively Fabricated Illusions by Eldon Taylor - a philosophical primer for the loss of and search for God.

Thinking Without Thinking by Eldon Taylor - required reading if you want to live in the present, a "free soul in a free world."

The Guides by William Guillory - channeled by a college professor, chair of the department of chemistry. This book must be read!

The Little Black Book by Eldon Taylor - an amazing little book that says it all. Consciousness just is and reality is relative to relationships.

Wellness: Just A State Of Mind by Eldon Taylor - This book goes a step beyond the so called mind-body connection. Do we choose our dis-ease? Can we "un-choose."

Simple Things And Simple Thoughts by Eldon Taylor - if thoughts are atomic, this book is nuclear energy compacted into a few words.

Subliminal Learning by Eldon Taylor - How do we learn behaviors and why are some habits so hard to change?

Subliminal Communication by Eldon Taylor - at last the truth about subliminal communication. Are you being subliminally manipulated?

FOR MORE INFORMATION

R. K. Books is the publishing imprint of Progressive Awareness, a company dedicated to providing the finest tools and information for "awakening" the spirit.

Together, R. K. Books and Progressive Awareness publish over 300 books and audio tapes. If you would like a free catalogue, please write to:

Progressive Awareness
557 California St., Suite 118
Boulder City, NV
89005

or telephone:

1-800-964-3551

R.K. Books
"For books that ***do*** *something."*

and

Progressive Awareness Research,
producers of InnerTalk™ tapes
"When believing in yourself matters!"